Daughter of Isis

Joanna Makepeace

D1506610

**G.K. Hall & Co. • Chivers Press
Thorndike, Maine USA Bath, England**

This Large Print edition is published by G.K. Hall & Co., USA
and by Chivers Press, England.

Published in 1997 in the U.S. by arrangement with Margaret
York.

Published in 1997 in the U.K. by arrangement with the author.

U.S. Softcover   0-7838-2017-8   (Paperback Collection Edition)
U.K. Hardcover   0-7451-8902-4   (Chivers Large Print)

The text of this Large Print edition is unabridged.
Other aspects of the book may vary from the original edition.

Set in 16 pt. Bookman Old Style.

Printed in the United States on permanent paper.

British Library Cataloguing in Publication Data available

Library of Congress Cataloging in Publication Data

Makepeace, Joanna.
   Daughter of Isis / Joanna Makepeace.
     p.   cm.
   ISBN 0-7838-2017-8 (lg. print : sc)
   1. Princesses — Egypt — Fiction. 2. Large type books. I. Title.
[PR6063.A359D3 1997]
823'.914—dc21   96-45046

For my father,
John Edward York

AUTHOR'S NOTE

The characters and events of this book are fictitious. The names Ramoses and Mern-ptah and Asenath carry no historical or biblical significance and do not relate to any actual persons bearing such names.

JOANNA MAKEPEACE

1

Asenath stared down at the ornamental fish with a little pout of dissatisfaction. Indeed, she could not have said why. They were very beautiful. The sun's rays slanted down on them making them gleam as if composed of the molten gold which Geb worked so intricately in his shop near the river, skilfully fashioning the necklaces and bracelets she loved to wear. A few yards away a little group of her companions were giggling over a love poem. Nowadays they seemed to be able to think of nothing else. Merit was waving the papyrus scroll her lover had contrived to give her at the feast last night, when her mother's back had been turned.

It was not in Asenath's nature to sulk for long and she laughed as she re-joined them and expertly flicked the scroll from her friend's hand then began to read it aloud.

'Oh Princess,' gasped the embarrassed girl. 'Please don't. We might be overheard.'

'But I thought you wanted everyone to know,' Asenath teased her.

'Please, Princess. If my mother heard, she would be furious.'

7

'Why, it seems a good match?'

'And what, Lady,' grated Mem-net, 'would you know about such matters?'

'I have big ears,' retorted Asenath, 'or so my brothers say.'

'Your brother will be returning from Kush shortly,' Mem-net said, and not for the first time Asenath thought she could detect an odd quality of tone in her voice that she did not quite like.

'It will be good to have the Prince at court again,' sighed pretty Nefertari. She was a cousin to the Royal children, since her father, Raban ben Zareth, was brother to Pharaoh's Royal Wife, Asenath's dearly loved stepmother. Asenath had great affection for the girl who was two years her junior, but she felt irritated by the silly chit's worship of her elder brother.

'You have a Royal Prince present at court,' she said sharply. 'My brother, Hotep-Re, has never been away.'

'But Mern-ptah is so handsome and he is the Royal Heir.'

'That has yet to be decided,' Asenath snapped.

'The deciding will be done by your Royal Father,' Mem-net countered firmly, 'so let us have no nonsense when you greet him, Lady.'

Asenath knew well why she dreaded the return of her brother, though she refused to put it into words. One day her father, Pharaoh himself, would summon her to his apartment to order her to marry the Royal Heir. All Egypt knew it would be Mern-ptah but Asenath wished passionately that it were not so. It had never been spoken, but well she knew she was Throne Princess of The Two Lands and the Royal Heir must become her husband. It mattered little that the young companions who formed her circle thought her the most fortunate woman in Egypt. Since she herself was not of their opinion, it was no comfort.

Asenath was almost sixteen. Her nurse, Mem-net, regarded her charge with stern affection. She would soon be in the full flush of her beauty and already showed signs of loveliness inherited from her lovely dead mother, the Lady Ashtar, who had come as a gift to Pharaoh from her father the King of Syria. She had died bearing this wilful, passionate child, but the baby had never lacked affection for she was the darling of both Pharaoh and his Royal Wife, the Lady Serana. Asenath was as deeply loved as if she had been Serana's daughter in fact, and she was spoiled by her Royal Father, who denied her nothing. She leaned back on the bench, her full under lip thrust out in a petulant expression of defiance. Her dusky skin was smooth and radiant with health and the dark hair which glinted with a hint of copper, flowed unrestrained down her back, ornamented only with a single band of beaten gold. The grey eyes were a little stormy now and she stared down in haughty disdain at the nurse for whom she normally held a wealth of respect and affection.

The elder of Pharaoh's sons was at present leading a punitive expedition into Kush. Though only just past seventeen, he had already proved himself an able officer and, as he was now accompanied by Pharaoh's most trusted general, Men-ophar, no one doubted his ability to deal with the situation, and daily news was expected from him that he would shortly be home. He had become a favourite with the court ladies but Asenath found her half-brother's arrogance infuriating. She could not have said why the thought of him brought fear to her heart. They had had their quarrels as children but he had never sought to harm her. Indeed he had hardly appeared to notice her at all.

Her younger brother, Hotep-Re, was gentle and scholarly, and though he too had been trained in the Prince's School and could hold his own in the art of wrestling and shooting, he did not scorn to spend an occasional hour with his half-sister talking of poetry and art. He was growing tall and handsome now though almost a year younger than her, but in appearance, he rather resembled his lovely mother than his fierce proud father who was Pharaoh of The Two Lands.

He came now into the garden and Asenath's lips parted in a smile of greeting and the girls made gestures of respect as he approached.

'Welcome my brother. Hotep-Re spare me a moment of your time and come and talk to me. No,' she said sharply as her nurse rose at once to accompany them, 'I shall not need you yet, Mem-net.'

The nurse sat back discomfited. Hotep-Re remarked on it as they crossed the grass.

'You hurt her and she loves you.'

'Why can't she shower all her care on you, you are the baby.'

'Asenath, I am a man grown. Mem-net relinquished her hold on me, long ago.'

Asenath pouted. 'Why should men always have their own way? No one respects my wishes.'

He laughed. 'Everyone in the royal palace defers to them, from our Royal Father, down to the meanest slave in the household, when you do not sulk that is. What is wrong with you lately?'

'Nothing — what do you mean?'

'You seem irritated. Are you worried about something?'

In her bedroom she kicked off her sandals

11

and threw herself on to the bed while he sat opposite. 'No, I don't think so, just growing pains. Ptah Hoten says they are, at any rate.'

He grinned in answer. 'A very painful disease. I have felt its ravages often.'

She propped her head on her bent arm as she gazed moodily round the lovely room. 'Where have you been most of the day?' she enquired, her voice still carrying the note of petulance he had noted recently. It disturbed him, for previously his sister had had a sunny, winning nature and he had deep affection for her.

'I went wildfowling early with some friends. The sport was good — the cats enjoyed it.'

'You did not?'

'No. I appear to have an odd distaste for killing and maiming living things,' he shrugged, 'at any rate my friends consider it odd.'

'Mern-ptah considers it odd, but then, you are not alike.'

'We are alike in essentials.'

'Are you fond of Mern-ptah?'

'Of course.'

'You wouldn't wish to upset him in any way?'

'Well of course I would not,' he grinned again broadly, 'it wouldn't pay me to, either.'

'You are afraid of him?'

'I wouldn't put it as strongly as that. He's just bigger than I am.'

'Don't you sometimes wish you were the elder?'

'I don't think so — perhaps. At times all children wish that.'

'And you haven't considered the succession?' She got up abruptly and moved to the open window, her back to him.

He frowned deliberately, an action which showed him clearly as his father's son. 'There is no question of the succession. Though no official statement has been issued, Father expects Mern-ptah to succeed him. You know that.'

She swung round and he noticed that her eyes glittered unnaturally. 'But *I* am Throne Princess. Whoever marries me takes the double crown. What if I prefer you?'

He threw back his head and laughed. 'So you would set brother against brother. . . . No, Asenath, I am not your man.'

'I could be happy with you.'

'Because you think you would get more of your own way. You could be mistaken.'

'We understand one another. We like the same things. I love you, Hotep-Re, as a true brother.'

'And I am fond of you, but I think this conversation has gone quite far enough. Can you imagine our father's rage if it were

13

relayed to him?'

'He has not finally chosen and he loves me. He would listen.'

'On this matter, no. He has decided. His choice was made long ago. I am quite content,' his lips tightened, 'you are never to refer to this again. I am no coward, but I dread to think of Mern-ptah's anger. Do not seek to come between us Asenath. For this, I would hate you. Now I must go.'

She moved to detain him. 'Dear Hotep-Re, do not be angry. You know I love you well — I but teased you.'

He turned and faced her directly. 'Such teasing is below the dignity of a Princess of The Two Lands. I *would* be angry if I did not think you seriously unhappy, my sister. You must come to terms with your destiny as we all must. Think on what I have said, but do not fear, I shall never even think about what you have said. It will leave my mind as if your lips had never uttered the thought.' Bending, he lightly kissed her forehead and left the room.

She made no effort to prevent him, but stood, tight-lipped and silent until the patter of his sandals ceased to sound in the corridor, then she turned and snatched at a dark cloak which hung on the wall and hurriedly followed him. In the corridor she encountered a huge Nubian whose face expressed concern as he saw her robed to

14

leave the palace. She imperiously gestured to him to attend her.

'Boda, I go to the Temple of Ptah. Accompany me.' He followed her at a suitable distance. She knew she would be perfectly safe with the Negro slave as his massive form was trained in combat and she feared no attacker. In childhood, when he had been captured, he had been rendered dumb by the simple removal of his tongue. Kindness and consideration he received as a palace slave had made his devotion sure and his affection for the children of his master was almost dog-like.

The streets were crowded with craftsmen returning home from their labours. Knowing that Boda followed at a safe distance, she hurried past them until she reached the pylon of the Temple of Ptah, passed under the gate and entered the outer courtyard. From the Temple itself she could hear the hymn of the evening celebration, the sound of chanting and the tinkle of the systra of the priestesses. She longed to enter but something seemed to hold her back and she leaned her forehead against the cold stone in desperation. Most of the visitors had left the Temple precincts; the priests of this Temple were healers and ministered to the sick of the city, but their work of the day was over, so there was none to see her weakness save Boda, who withdrew a distance and stood like a massive black statue with his arms folded, awaiting her pleasure.

She knew it was Ptah Hoten who placed his arm round her shoulder and made little effort to hide from him her distress. The serene beauty of the High Priest's face was as familiar to her as those of her own family and she allowed him to lead her gently to his apartments. He made no comment but waited quietly for her to speak.

'Don't ask me what is wrong, Ptah Hoten, I don't think I really know,' she said at last.

He spread his palms upwards on his desk and smiled. 'Why should you need a reason?'

'For crying?'

'Was that what you were doing?'

She flushed and looked down at the floor. 'I have quarrelled with Hotep-Re.'

'That is indeed strange.'

She sighed. 'I have quarrelled recently with almost everyone in the palace. What is wrong with me, Ptah Hoten?'

He smiled. 'I think you regret the leaving behind of childhood, though you will not admit it.'

'You mean that *before* I didn't see all the evil things around me, but they were there all the same?'

'Something like that.'

She shivered and standing up moved to

run her fingers lovingly over a small statue of the God, which stood on a carved chest. 'His face is calm and beautiful, but I wish he were not pictured in the grave clothes.'

'Life and form are one, Asenath. Have I taught you so little that you do not know that?'

'I know it,' her voice was low. 'My mother died in giving me life, did she not?'

'That is true, but child you must not fear. It is not likely to happen to you. Asenath, look at me, is this what frightens you?'

She came back to him slowly. 'I don't know what frightens me, Ptah Hoten, but I do not want to be married. Please, you must help me. I cannot bear to think of it. Would you accept me as a priestess? I could be at peace here I know it. My father could not force me if I told him I was dedicated to the worship of the gods. He would have to let me train first. It would give me time.'

He took her chilled fingers in his own. 'Child, this is sheer panic. You cannot fly to the gods as a refuge from life. That is no service. Can she who is afraid to marry and bear a child hope to be initiated, conquer herself and her bodies and her will? You are a daughter of the gods. You cannot hope to escape your duty by hiding in the sanctuary.'

She turned from him, her lips trembling. 'I did not ask to be born daughter of Pharaoh,' she said in a piteous whisper. And as he forbore to answer, she swung round and peered into his face.

'Of that I can say nothing. Duty always seems hard to the young. You would find your fate no easier to bear had you been born into slavery. You have much to thank the gods for. You have been dearly loved, Asenath. Take my advice and talk this out with the Royal Wife or your father.'

She smiled bleakly. 'One does not talk things out with my Royal Father, Ptah Hoten and well you know it.'

He nodded. 'Yet he loves you well. Tell me, is it Mern-ptah you fear?'

'Yes.'

'But I do not understand. You have always played happily together in the past. Has he been unkind to you?'

'No.' She turned away. 'I have seen little of him recently. When he is at court he hardly notices me.'

'Many girls are given in marriage knowing nothing of their future husbands. You at least know that yours will be honourable and thoughtful of your welfare.'

'Do I?' A bitter little smile twisted her lips. 'Ptah Hoten I have spoken of this to no one but you. You will keep my secret. My father has not spoken of marriage yet, but I feel that it will be soon now.'

He inclined his head once, then as she

rose escorted her to the door where Boda waited. 'It is late. I feel you should return to the palace before you are missed.'

As Asenath hurried through the palace gardens to reach her own apartments she was called, and, turning, saw the Royal Wife standing in the doorway of her own room.

'Asenath, is that you?'

'Yes, my mother.' The girl turned a little guiltily. She was conscious that her tears had left her face somewhat smudged and swollen and hoped her stepmother would not notice.

'Child it is late. Have you been out?'

'Yes, I visited the Temple of Ptah. I had Boda with me, I was not unattended. I went to evening celebrations.'

'You must let Mem-net know of your intentions. She was concerned about you, and so was I.'

'I am sorry I have displeased you.'

'Child, I love you.' Serana tilted up the lovely face and smiled. 'You know we worry if you are out without guards. But no more of that — come into my room for a moment. I have something to tell you.'

Asenath obeyed thankfully. She checked for a moment at the disarray in the room. The ladies had opened chest after chest and dresses and jewelry lay in heaps on the floor.

'Now you can help me as you are here. What shall I wear at the feast tomorrow?'

Asenath knelt and mechanically began to sort among the delicate fabrics. 'Blue I think for you, or green, both seem to bring out the colour of your eyes. But why the interest? Do we honour some important dignitary?'

'Did you not hear?'

'No, my mother.'

'Mern-ptah will be home tomorrow. He is victorious. The royal barge should arrive by noon and Pharaoh will honour his son by a royal banquet. Choose your loveliest gown, Asenath. It will be a happy and glittering occasion. I am so happy. It will be wonderful to have him home again.'

Asenath held up a necklace studded with lapis. She avoided her stepmother's eyes. 'Wear this with the pale blue, my mother. It is father's favourite. Tomorrow you will look as young as the day Mern-ptah was born.'

2

Mern-ptah put up a be-ringed hand to hide his yawn. He stole a surreptitious glance at his general, Men-ophar, and gave an inward grin at the man's stony disapproving countenance. The performance of the slave girls left little to the imagination. He gave a slight curl of the lips which indicated his distaste at the scene around him. The Hittite ambassador on his left was unaware of his contempt. He was breathing fatuous, drunken comments into the ear of the girl on his knees.

The Hittite ambassador had a pleasure villa situated within a day's sailing of Thebes. He had been delighted to offer hospitality to the elder son of Pharaoh. He had set aside for the young prince a fine apartment and the entertainment he offered was of the choicest. Most of the guests had partaken of it too well, and by this time were hardly aware of their surroundings.

Mern-ptah drank sparingly and the drunken maundering of the foreign dignitary offended his fastidious nature. The campaign had been hard and he was anxious now to press on to Thebes and make his report. Tonight it would have pleased him more to retire early, so as to make an early start the next day, but he knew better than to offend foreign dignitaries and he smiled, though coldly, and gave polite attention to his host's conversation.

Though still slim, his body was perfectly proportioned. His muscles rippled under his tanned, oiled skin, which was set off by his simple though rich kilt of blue pleated linen. His plaited youth lock was ornamented with gold and a pectoral of turquoise and lapis lazuli lay across the broad smooth chest. Not for the first time, General Men-ophar cast an admiring glance at him. The broad commanding brow was like his father's, and beneath, the proud black eyes bore an expression of sleepy indifference. Once or twice Men-ophar had noticed a flash of fire, which showed the other's anger; when the deformed acrobat's performance had been greeted by yells of derision, and again when a young slave girl had moved quickly away to avoid the demanding clutch of a guest's greasy fingers. He was the child of Ramoses, even to that beautiful, almost childlike mouth which saved the proud face from a first impression of cold cruelty. The young prince could be judged arrogant, wilful and demanding, but the tenderness of that mouth spoke of an understanding and sympathetic nature which was not deep below the surface.

Men-ophar was pleased by the boy's performance. He had shown dash and courage and enough youthful confidence to be impatient of advice, but he was no fool and Men-ophar's wisdom had never been completely disregarded, and not once had he displayed anything but respect and politeness for the older man's authority. The rebellion had been competently put down and the cavalry detachment had seen enough to assure them of their young prince's ability to command. His Royal Father would be well pleased.

The Hittite ambassador slapped his companion smartly on the buttocks and as she squealed, dropped her protesting to the floor. He stood up drunkenly, and shouted for the attendant slave to refill his goblet.

'We hope you are enjoying our hospitality, Prince Mern-ptah,' he said, his voice slurred with wine, 'but we cannot send you to a cold bed.'

The Hittite clumsily leaned forward in an owlish confidential manner, splashing wine on to the prince's bare arm.

'I am sure at your father's court they have already initiated you into the pleasures of love?' he said, chuckling hoarsely. 'But there are other delights. We may yet offer you a new experience.' He clapped his hands smartly and shouted to a Negro slave at attendance near the door. 'Bring me the girl, Taia.' He turned back to his guest. 'This is my great sacrifice to your comfort. The girl is new — only last week I acquired her — but she shall give you pleasure tonight. Mind you must be firm with her, I'll warrant there will be tears in plenty, but she already knows how to behave. I've seen to that.'

Mern-ptah was anxious to avoid offence. 'I could not deprive you of a choice possession. I assure you, I have been honoured enough.'

The doors opened and the slave pushed a diminutive figure ahead of him. Mern-ptah, determined to decline the offer, did not at first give the slave-girl a second glance, then as he turned, checked suddenly and stared down into the child's terrified eyes. She could have been no more than nine or ten years of age, but her face had been painted and her thin body adorned with transparent silk and jewelry. He saw at once that she was striving to keep back the tears, but she slipped to her knees before her master and kissed the thongs of his jewelled sandals. He fondled her hennaed hair, which fell forward on to her thinly-covered, childish breasts.

'See how she loves me. Listen Taia, you must put aside your desire for me tonight.' He gave a drunken laugh, as her shoulders heaved convulsively. 'For I command you to please this noble lord, who is my guest. Is he not handsome?' He tilted up her chin and Mern-ptah saw her flinch at his touch as if expecting a blow. 'He honours you mightily. See that you prove satisfactory.'

She stood up and turned blindly towards him, her head hanging low. Mern-ptah thought quickly. 'Now this,' he said huskily, 'I confess, is something new in my experience. She is very young indeed.'

He avoided the shocked gaze of Men-ophar, stood up and eased his cramped limbs. 'Will you have her conveyed to my apartments?'

The Hittite gave orders and the girl was led away. He put a companionable arm round the prince's shoulders and moved off with him. Mern-ptah was dimly aware that his general had risen and followed. At the door of his apartment, he released himself from the other's clutching hands and faced Men-ophar.

'See that I am not disturbed. I wish two guards to remain here and allow no one to enter nor are they to do so themselves on any pretext, unless I command it.'

With a last slap of encouragement, Mardok lurched off along the corridor.

Mern-ptah refused to catch his general's eye. Curtly bidding him, 'Good night,' he opened the door of his apartment, entered and firmly closed it behind him as an indication that he wished to say no more.

The girl turned at once at his entrance. Her black eyes opened wide as she scrutinised his face for signs which would allow her to assess his character. Child that she was, she had already some knowledge of men, but this young prince's expression of disdain offered no hope of mercy. She forced her painted lips to a travesty of a smile and slipped to her knees in an unchildish coquettish pose. Overwhelming pity welled inside him, warring with a feeling of sick disgust. He came to her and pulled her to her feet.

'Stand up, child. What is your name?'

'I am called Taia.'

'Then, Taia, you need not cringe. You have nothing to fear from me.'

The child regarded him wonderingly, then lowered her eyes again. 'I will try to please you,' she whispered.

He took her by the hand and led her to the bed. 'You do not understand me, child. I shall not touch you. How old are you?'

She shook her head. 'I do not know, lord. They said about nine years, in the slave market.'

'I guessed about that. Were you born in slavery?'

'Yes, lord. My mother was owned by a wealthy farmer with an estate near Tanis.

Some months ago my master died and my mistress sold the estate and nearly all the slaves. I was bought in the market for Mardok by his steward. I have only been here a little time.'

'I see.' Mern-ptah turned from her and swept up one of the luxurious cushions from the bed and a soft fur covering. He looked round for a suitable resting place, then dumped them on a low day couch near to the window. 'You can sleep here. Do not be afraid. You will be quite safe. No one will enter the room during the night. My soldiers have my orders.' He gave a tight-lipped smile. 'I assure you, they will not disobey.'

She swallowed and looked at the great bed. 'My lord, I . . .'

His smile broadened. 'I shall inform Mardok that you are a delight of delights or some such nonsense. He will suspect nothing.'

Her eyes filled with sudden tears, and hesitatingly she sat down on the couch. 'You are sure . . . I am not afraid.'

'Are you not?' he said quietly.

She made no answer and her eyes travelled to a low table near the bed. He had been provided with fruit, cakes and wine in case he awoke in the night and required refreshment.

'Are you hungry?' he asked.

27

'I am thirsty, lord. If I could have some water . . .'

He raised his eyebrows. 'Do they not feed you, child?'

She avoided his eyes. 'Mardok has not been pleased with me. He gives me drink when he is satisfied.'

'I begin to understand.' He splashed wine into a silver goblet and held it out to her. 'Eat some of the cakes. I shall require nothing.'

She came to his side and reached hesitatingly for the goblet then gulped thirstily. He waved her to the table for food and turned to the bed. As he made no movement whatever to further approach her, she gathered courage and ate her fill of the cakes and wine, then casting a quick look towards the ornate bed where he sprawled with a papyrus scroll, she tip-toed back to the couch and settled her thin body to unexpected rest.

She was awakened abruptly by someone shaking her shoulder hard. She started up in terror and stared into the black eyes of the Egyptian prince. It was full early, only grey light filtered in through the window, but he was already dressed.

'Get into my bed.' His demand was unmistakable and as she moved to obey but slowly, his tone hardened. 'Hurry now, remove your clothing and obey me.'

Now fully awake, she had learnt not to disobey and with shaking fingers, dropped her discarded clothing where he indicated and climbed into the huge bed. He threw the covers over her and smiled.

'I will order refreshment. Go back to sleep. I shall not disturb you.'

She cowered down into the luxurious cushions and watched while he threw open the door and called instructions to the guards outside.

When Men-ophar entered about half an hour later, his eyes flickered to the tiny figure of the child in the bed. Mern-ptah wiped sticky fingers on a kerchief and smiled at him sardonically.

'I trust you slept well, my lord.' The general's voice was polite but coldly formal.

'Excellently, I thank you. We *both* enjoyed ourselves, is that not so?' The mobile lips curved into a smile she had not imagined he would ever give, as he turned to include her in his answer. She nodded briefly and the general bowed.

'How soon will you wish to start, lord? Your Royal Father expects us by noon.'

'I shall be ready in less than an hour. I shall embark then. Will you attend to the arrangements?'

'Certainly, lord.' Men-ophar's disapproval could almost be felt like a physical blow, as he bowed low once more and withdrew.

Their host appeared somewhat sick and wan by the light of dawn, nevertheless he arrived to bid them a good journey.

'Your hospitality will long remain in my memory, Mern-ptah said smoothly. 'Pharaoh shall hear of your good wishes, my lord. One last favour I would ask.'

'Lord Prince, it is yours.'

'I would buy the child. She has pleased me well. Ask what price you will. It will be paid.'

The Hittite ambassador bowed almost to the ground. 'My lord, it will be my great pleasure to offer her as a slight remembrance of your stay. I will send the necessary documents to the barge.'

'You are most generous, my lord. I would be churlish to refuse. I hope we may receive you soon at Thebes or Per-Ramoses. I trust your stay there will be as pleasurable.' Mern-ptah turned his shoulder slightly. 'Convey the girl to my barge. Once again, my lord, I thank you in Pharaoh's name. May your gods prove kind,' and with a smile in the direction of his general, he moved from the villa and down to the landing stage.

Lolling under the shelter of the awning on a low couch, Mern-ptah idly watched the light gleam on the oiled bodies of the rowers as their arms moved rhythmically to their task and the barge moved steadily downstream. He began to hum under his breath a tune which had been popular in Thebes before his departure. He had heard Asenath singing it with their cousin Nefertari. Would Asenath be pleased to see him? He rather thought not. The girl had become sulky of late. He should have bought her some favour to sweeten her temper, but it had not crossed his mind until now. Near the prow of the boat, the little maid was sitting, her knees hunched up to her chin. In the full light of day, her tawdry clothing looked garish. The child had given him an idea. He turned and laughed as he caught Menophar's cold gaze which was hurriedly turned aside.

'Spare me your disapproval, General,' he said laughing, 'I have not touched the girl. Have you so little regard for me? Did you think me already so degenerate?'

The older man's face reddened darkly. 'My lord,' he said hurriedly, 'it is not for me to judge. It is just that . . .'

'Just so.' The wry twist to the lips was a gesture unconsciously copied from his Royal Father. 'Such treatment of a child is the action of a sadist — a perverted one at that. No, my good friend and adviser, I thought she would be happier resting on a couch in my room than in the arms of that drunken beast. Then it occurred to me that he might part with her and I did not think

31

it would be quite so easy.'

Men-ophar smiled. 'And now you are wondering what to do with her. Is that it?'

'Oh no.' Mern-ptah rose and stretched himself. 'I know what to do with her. I shall give her as a gift to my sister, Asenath.'

3

Asenath wished passionately for the hundredth time that day that ceremonial wigs had never been invented. She nodded her chin imperatively to the young Nubian slave who was fanning her with a huge fan of ostrich feathers. Her head ached abominably and the weight of the wig, surmounted by its elaborate headdress, increased her discomfort. She sighed, but only very softly. One did not allow Pharaoh to hear a subject express a feeling of misery on a ceremonial occasion such as this. She stole a glance at her Royal Father on the carved throne to her right.

In spite of the heat of noon, he was wearing the heavy double crown of the Two Lands, and held the crook and flail, symbols of his office, in his two hands. Not even the suspicion of a frown creased his brow and his proud face appeared god-like in its impassivity and he gazed serenely ahead. By his side sat the Royal Wife, Serana, for once her pale gold hair, so unusual at the Egyptian court, hidden beneath a wig as elaborate and uncomfortable as Asenath's own. She was dressed in a pleated robe of soft blue, her sandals studded with gold. She looked neither impassive nor uncomfortable. Her blue eyes were fixed on the broad expanse of river where at any moment, she would catch her first sight of the barge which would bring her elder son home. If only it would come, Asenath thought, we could get this ceremonial greeting over, and return to the shaded rooms of the palace. Hotep-Re grinned at her sympathetically. He had been spared a wig at least, but even he was sweating in this heat. She could see heavy drops forming on his upper lip. He too was straining his eyes to see the barge. Was she the only one who dreaded Mern-ptah's return?

The landing stage was crowded with court officials. Behind her father stood the High Priest of Ptah, Ptah Hoten, and next to him the steward of the royal household and the Grand Vizier, Nefren, her father's most trusted official and adviser. Everyone of importance in Thebes had been summoned to welcome the victorious prince home.

Along the river banks the work-people of Thebes pushed and jostled for vantage points. They were in holiday mood, chattering and laughing, delighted at the success of the young prince. A cheer was heard and taken up further up river. The barge was approaching. Even Asenath leaned forward in her seat expectantly.

As the great ship was made fast to the landing stage, the Ammon priests broke into a chant of thanksgiving for the success of the enterprise. Asenath could see her brother, waiting with Men-ophar to disembark. Just once he acknowledged the acclamation of the artisans and townsfolk with a wave of his hand. The sun truly shone on him today. Victory was his and he was young enough to enjoy it without regrets. He had taken only mild steps to punish the offenders; prisoners and slaves there were in plenty, but it was for Pharaoh to decide their fate. He sprang ashore as soon as it was possible to come before Pharaoh and salute him as a dutiful subject.

Pharaoh's voice was warm with affection. 'We are indeed proud to welcome you, my son. Already we have received news of your success.'

Mern-ptah bowed again. 'I think you will be well pleased, lord. I will give you a complete report when you wish. I have obeyed your wishes and taken the advice of Men-ophar as you commanded. He has guarded me well and been a kind adviser. He has spared my mistakes I am sure, in his own reports.'

Pharaoh smiled graciously at his general. 'Welcome home, Men-ophar. You will be glad to reach Thebes.'

The general prostrated himself and withdrew. Pharaoh indicated his wife. 'I am sure, my son, your mother waits to greet you and your brother and sister.'

Serana enfolded her son in her arms. He drew away and put a light finger to a tear which glimmered on her cheek. 'Dear one, I was never in any danger. Men-ophar saw to that.'

'My son, I have many times known the worth of General Men-ophar. My tears are a mark of my joy that all is well with you.' She let him go, though her arms yearned to keep him close to her side. It seemed impossible that it was seventeen years since Ptah Hoten had first placed him there. Now her head did not reach his shoulder and he would soon be as broad and powerful as his father. Hotep-Re gripped his brother's arms beaming with pleasure and squealed as Mern-ptah punched him affectionately in the waist. Officials murmured polite expressions of congratulation and the party round the throne began to move.

At last the bearers lifted the chairs of Pharaoh and the Royal Wife on to their shoulders and prepared to carry them to the Great House. A young groom handed the reins of a light gilded chariot to the elder prince and he turned and threw out one hand towards Asenath.

'Will you accompany me home, little sister?'

It was almost as regal a command as their father's but Asenath bowed her head and made no comment as he drew her up, and she braced herself for the drive.

'You look most grown up and beautiful, my sister,' he said as they moved off. 'Even the heat appears not to disturb you.'

'My brother is gracious,' she said a trifle coldly. 'I am honoured to drive with the victor.'

'I seem to have seen little of you recently.'

'I think you have been occupied with affairs of greater moment,' she said her eyes fixed straight ahead. 'Was your journey pleasant?'

He made a rueful face, turning briefly to glance at her as he skilfully turned his team into the avenue of sphinxes which led to the palace. 'Pleasant but uneventful. I shall be pleased to reach home and have my own slaves attend me. I am glad we are at Thebes, not in the Delta. I wish to see Ptah Hoten and visit the Temple.'

Conversation was brought to an end as he drew the chariot to a halt and grooms flew to the horses' heads. He assisted her to step down, then was engulfed by the arms of a half hysterical Mem-net who launched herself at him, laughing and crying at once. Asenath stood a little uncertainly as he stooped and kissed his nurse while laughingly replying to her admonitions and expressions of concern about the dangers he had encountered. He flung his arm round her and drew her within the palace. Asenath was apparently forgotten. With a small gasp of annoyance she flung off to her own apartments to wait for some lessening of the heat before the lengthy preparations for the evening's festivities.

Her temper was not improved when she found a little knot of servants giggling in her room. She caught the phrase, 'slave girl' and 'prince', then the laughter was abruptly hushed at her approach.

Her tone was petulant as she was exasperated and tired. 'Don't stand and stare at me, idle ones. Get off about your work. Neri — you stay and take off this wretched wig and the jewelry. The whole outfit is weighing me down and I have a terrible headache.'

The women stared at her like sheep, and she was tempted to slap one, but she resisted the urge, and as the older girl moved to obey her and lift the cumbersome headdress from her aching brows, she ordered the rest curtly to leave her. This time they did not wait, but seeing signs of anger darkening her grey eyes, they quickly withdrew and she frowned as their high giggles and chattering could still be heard in the corridor outside her door. She kicked off her sandals and stripped off the golden necklace which would cut into her throat and shoulders and threw herself on to the bed. Neri brought her rose water and bathed her throbbing temples.

'What were they talking about?' she asked the slave. 'I thought I heard a reference to my brother. Did they mean Prince Mernptah?'

The girl flushed and lowered her head. 'They are young and very foolish, Princess. They listen to gossip. You should not be angry with them. They mean no harm.'

'Gossip — what gossip?'

'The prince is handsome and they are glad to see his return.'

'Nonsense, Neri. You are evading the question. Why the giggles?' She caught at the girl's bare arm. 'I swear I will slap you hard, if you do not tell me at once.'

The girl hesitated then burst out, 'They say he has brought back a pretty girl slave of his own. She pleased him so much he tried to buy her from Mardok the Hittite, but he was given the girl as a gift.'

Asenath's tone was cold. 'The prince's affairs are not their concern. You may leave me now. Neri,' she called sharply, as the girl bowed and made to withdraw, 'tell Mem-net she is not to enter. I am tired. I will sound the gong when I am ready to dress for the feast.'

In spite of Asenath's irritation that so much adulation was being heaped on her elder brother, she was woman-like enough to dress becomingly for the feast. Her robe was of lilac coloured mist linen, fine as gossamer and her bracelets and necklace were studded with dark amethysts, a present from her stepmother. She fanned herself vigorously with a delicate framework of pale pink ostrich feathers set on an ivory handle, and pouted as she watched Mernptah's progress down the hall.

He certainly was looking his best — in a kilt of gold metallic weave, his only ornament a delicate chain bearing the golden wings of the falcon god, Horus. He was relating some anecdote to two young cavalry officers and their expressions showed their amusement. She averted her eyes and beckoned to a slave to bring her refreshment.

Half way through the festivities, Asenath signalled to a young fan-bearer, and stepped out into the scented garden for welcome coolness. The slave walked behind at a respectful distance and she moved along under the flowering oleander, her shimmering skirts brushing the scarlet lilies and flowering shrubs. Behind her the sound of revelry, blended with shrieks of laughter and muffled giggles, told her that she was not the only guest to seek the peace of the gardens. She walked down to the ornamental pool and sat down on a marble bench, idly tapping her foot to the music of the blind harper which carried faintly but still audibly, from the Hall of Audience.

'Seeking peace, Princess?'

She looked up startled as she had not thought to have been followed, then smiled as she recognised the intruder. Rehorem-heb the master builder, was a welcome friend at court and had often soothed her tempers or solaced her when hurt. She silently invited him to join her on the bench, and they sat still for a moment in companionable silence watching the fish glide under the silvered leaves of the lotus flowers.

'It is beautiful here now,' she said at last. 'It has been so hot today, my head has ached and I felt if I stayed with another crowd, I would go mad. Oh, Rehoremheb, I don't want another person — not one — to tell me how wonderful Mern-ptah is.'

He laughed and drew her back against his shoulder. 'Then I shall not add my praises or I will be dismissed from the presence of my favourite princess. Why so churlish, Asenath, it is not like you?'

'No,' she said thoughtfully, 'I was not liable to such prickliness — oh I am glad it was successful, but he is so vain. Tonight he seems to have become a giant, god-like in his achievements, more arrogant than Pharaoh himself.'

He shook his head. 'Just a boy proud of his accomplishments. When my first temple was built, I was unbearable — truly.'

'I cannot imagine you unbearable, dear Rehoremheb, you always seem to have mastery over your temper. Why did you never marry — you are so handsome I would have thought all Egypt would have been at your feet?' She glanced quickly at him, then as the light shone on his suddenly saddened face, she reached out and took his hand. 'I have been tactless, please forget I asked that. You have your own reasons.'

'A very lovely reason,' he said stroking her slim fingers.

'She did not love you?'

'Yes, she loved me, but our marriage was not — possible.'

'I am sorry. You sometimes see her?'

He shook his head. 'She died — long ago. Do not pity us, child. We were very happy. The Gods cannot give more than the short ecstasy I had. I do not ever ask for more.'

'No, if I could have that, I would not ask for more.'

'Asenath, you *will* have it. All your life is open before you.'

She stood up and looked down into the

pool. 'What life? Do you call it living to be cooped up in the harem — never to be free, never to know love?'

'My child' — he was concerned by her cry of pain which sprang from an overladen heart — 'you will be Queen of Egypt, no harem-slave.'

'What does it matter what title I bear? I shall be a slave, the property of Pharaoh. Oh, Rehoremheb — I don't want to marry Mern-ptah, I don't want to marry anyone.' He held her against his chest while she struggled for mastery over her tears. It would never do for her to re-enter the hall with black eye paint in smudges on her skilfully painted face.

'Is it determined?'

'It must be so. My father has not yet made it public or informed me that I must obey him in this, but I know his heart. He has made his decision. There is no escape.'

'And this makes you very unhappy?'

She nodded, and when she spoke again her voice was once more calm. 'Sometimes I feel like a painted bird beating its wings against the cage bars. I cannot be resigned to my duty like the others. Hotep-Re is content, Mern-ptah does not ask to live away from the restrictions of the court, and for all the power he will wield, he can never be free and he knows it. Even little Nefertari is quite content that some man should own her, and order her life, but I cannot accept it. I want to travel and see all The Two Lands. I want to work like Sen-u-ret and feel tired but happy because of a job well done, I want to have babies with a man who truly loves me, not with a brother who honours me only that he might wear the double crown. Is it so much to ask?'

'It is too much for *you* to ask, my little one.'

She sighed. 'I know it — it is only that sometimes my spirit rebels. You knew my mother, Rehoremheb. They tell me I am like her. Did she hate her life here?'

'No, I do not think she did entirely. She had no more choice than you. Her father sent her as a gift to Pharaoh.'

'Did he love her? Are you sure?'

'Yes, I believe that he did.'

'The lady Serana tells me that he did. It is strange that they were true friends. She loves my father so deeply, that had I been in her place, I would have hated his other women. Rehoremheb, I do not want to share my man with anyone — and I must.'

He tilted up her chin, his grey eyes gently ironic. 'You have much to learn, little one. Try to accept your life. Mern-ptah is a fine man, and will be a good ruler. He will need you. In your wisdom and companionship, he will find the hidden reserves of strength needed to rule The Two Lands. Egypt demands this of you. Can you not find your happiness in this knowledge?'

'I don't know.' Her voice was very low. 'I don't know, Rehoremheb. I pray Isis to grant me courage. Every day and night of my life I do that.'

The dancing girls were entertaining the company, as they re-entered the hall, so she did not think her absence had been remarked upon. Nevertheless she flushed under the scrutiny of her father's fierce black eyes as she returned to the royal dais.

'You were walking in the garden?'

'Yes, lord — but not unattended.'

'What kept you?'

'Rehoremheb came out and we talked together.'

Pharaoh's harsh frown relaxed. If she had been with Rehoremheb, she was safe enough.

'So that is where you were. I looked for you, my sister.'

Asenath turned to find Mern-ptah smiling down at her. She fanned herself to hide her annoyance. Was she to answer to everyone in the family each time she ventured out of sight?

'I have a present for you.'

She checked the vigorous movement of her hand and looked up at him, surprised.

'Mardok the Hittite made me a gift of one of his slaves. I thought her a suitable personal maid for you, my sister.'

'You thought her what?' Angry colour flooded her face and she stood up, determined to face him at her full height.

'How dare you say this to me. You bring back a girl you honoured with your favour.' The words were deliberately insulting. 'And then see fit to place her in my apartments to spy on me I suppose. I suggest, brother, you try such tactics on someone less perceptive.'

His eyebrows swept up and he put out a hand to stay her as she moved to fling past him. Angrily she shook him off and turned her head as she felt furious tears spring to her eyes.

'My Royal Father will excuse me — I think I shall be better alone for a while.'

Pharaoh's voice grated with anger as he coldly dismissed her and she knew explanations would be demanded of her later, but she was so angry she did not even fear punishment but rushed blindly from the room, not even stopping to observe Serana's exclamation of concern, or conscious of the startled glances and whispers of court officials.

Once in her own apartment, she struggled to stop herself from breaking down completely and ignoring the wonder in the eyes of her startled women, sharply ordered Mem-net to dismiss them.

'My head aches again. Get rid of them all.'

Mem-net was used to Asenath's rages. She knew the signs. The girl had made a scene, obviously. Unless she were very fortunate, she would feel her father's displeasure in the morning. It was useless now to chide her. Her lower lip was beginning to tremble and soon she would weep. It was for her old nurse to comfort her now and settle her for the night. She shooed the women out immediately.

'Dear Mem-net, do not be cross with me. I have made a scene before the court and my father is furious. With good reason — it was unforgivable but I could not stop myself.'

'Child, whatever has happened to upset you so?'

'My royal brother honours me with his cast-off slave girl. How dare he give her to me before all the court as if I were a green child? My ladies were sniggering about her the moment he arrived in Thebes.'

Mem-net gently drew her charge away and held her at arm's length.

'You are talking of the girl he has sent to you as a gift?'

'She is here?'

Mem-net nodded. 'One of the guards delivered her about an hour ago. Her name is Taia.'

'Indeed.' Asenath showed white teeth in a

cruel little smile. 'Since she is mine, I can deal with her.' She seized the bronze striker and struck the gong near her bed. 'Send the girl to me, Mem-net. She is a new acquisition. She must be taught obedience. Down in the guard room she will learn that it is not wise to spy upon Pharaoh's daughter.'

Mem-net shrugged helplessly and went into the outer room. It was only on odd occasions that this lovely child revealed the cruel streak in her nature, and then it was useless to plead for the victims of her displeasure. It was customary in Egyptian households to have new slaves whipped, but it rarely happened now in the palace, since the Royal Wife, the Lady Serana, openly showed her disapproval of such harsh practices and it was well known that Pharaoh was loth to go against her wishes in the matter.

When Boda entered he showed frank surprise at his mistress's orders. 'Take this new slave of mine to the guard room and give her ten lashes. I wish her to receive the customary schooling. See it is done and return her to me, here.'

He bowed and stared over her head at Mem-net, who drew the girl by the hand into the princess's apartment. Asenath swung round, then stopped and stared, her lips parting in amazement. The harem

48

slaves had stripped Taia of her tawdry finery and washed the paint from her child's face. She now wore a plain tunic of coarse linen and the copper arm bracelet all palace slaves wore on their left arms. Her pathetic thinness and the bruises upon her upper arms were fully revealed by the glow of the oil lamp on the writing table. She smiled suddenly, an expression of pure joy and ran forward, prostrating herself before the princess in utter abasement. Over her bent head, Asenath stared at Mem-net, then signalled to Boda to leave.

'Go, Boda, I do not think my orders will prove necessary,' she said quietly. 'You may leave the girl with me.' Avoiding her nurse's eye, she moved to a chair and bade the new slave rise. 'So you are Taia,' she said briskly. 'Stand up, child. My brother has spoken to me of you. I had not thought you so young. How old are you?'

'Nine years, lady. I hope you will be pleased with me. He commanded me to serve you well. You are his sister?'

'That is so. He tells me you are a gift from Mardok.'

'He asked for me.'

'Indeed?' Asenath's tone was cold.

'My lady, I worship him. He has been so kind. Mardok made me . . .' the child swallowed, 'he commanded me to please the prince.'

'I trust you did so.'

'He did not ask anything of me, lady. I slept on a couch in his room . . . and . . . when he knew . . . about . . . about Mardok, he asked to buy me, but Mardok was pleased to honour him and gave me freely as a gift.'

Asenath turned to Mem-net. 'Find the child somewhere to sleep. Tomorrow she can begin her training. I am sure she will do very well.' She hesitated. 'I must send my brother my grateful thanks in the morning.'

As the nurse drew the child into the corridor, she lay down on the bed and clutching to her a silken cushion, hit it again and again with her fists, until her frustration was expelled and uncontrollable tears rained down, marking the rich silk with black splodges of water mingled with eye-paint. How could she have been such a childish fool? Everyone would be laughing at her — and her father! She shuddered suddenly, as she thought of the courage she would need during her interview with him. When Mem-net re-entered, she reached out blindly for her nurse's comforting arms and sobbed out her grief and anger on the familiar shoulder.

4

When her father's personal attendant, Ach-
med, visited her early the next day, and
informed her gravely that her father wished
to see her in his private apartments after
the Hour of Audience, Asenath received the
news with a gracious smile, though inwardly
her heart thudded uncomfortably. Many
times in the past, such a summons had
resulted in severe punishment, and knowing her father's insistence on decorum at
all times and particularly on public occasions, it seemed hardly likely that he would
overlook such a scene as she had caused
the previous evening. She adored the handsome but stern man who was her father and
Lord of all Egypt, but she feared his anger,
as did all the members of his household. He
spared his children no less than he did his
slaves, and more than once she had cried
herself to sleep because the whipping he
had himself inflicted, had made it impossible to rest in a comfortable position.

She went to her favourite spot in the
garden and sat for a while staring at the
goldfish as they darted and gleamed in the

sunlight. Confined as they were in this small pool, they seemed content with their lot. If only she could become resigned. She envied them their placidity then rose at last with a sigh, realising that the dread time could not be put off for long. The Hour of Audience would soon end, and it would be unwise to further anger her father by keeping him waiting. She turned unwilling steps back towards the palace.

It was peaceful in the garden, and she was startled and angry when her arm was suddenly caught and Mern-ptah stepped from a side path to confront her, jerking her angrily to face him.

'So, my sister, it seems a convenient time to talk un-disturbed.' She wrenched at his fingers which clenched cruelly over her wrist, striving to free herself.

'Let me go — you are hurting me.'

He put his head close to her own, his black eyes snapping with anger. 'It is nothing to what I will do to you, if you dare to anger me so again.'

She threw back her head and stared back at him. All fear had fled, she was coldly furious.

'I had every right to be angry when you offer me in public your cast-off woman.'

'Do not talk such nonsense. Taia is but a child. Do you think me a degenerate lecher?'

'I did not know she was such a child.'

'Child or no — it makes no difference. Sooner or later you will receive in public the women I choose to favour, and you will learn to do it graciously.'

She at last forced off his fingers. 'I would rather die than become your wife,' she spat at him, unable to walk away as he barred her path.

'So trite a phrase my sister — and just as meaningless. Your death would serve no purpose; your marriage to me is unfortunately necessary.'

'Father has not yet declared it so — he will not — he cannot do it — when I am so unhappy.' She gulped back the tears which she was determined he should not have the satisfaction of seeing.

Once more he caught her, this time by both shoulders, and his hands bit into her soft flesh marking it cruelly. 'Listen to me, Asenath, I shall become The Royal Heir and you will be wise to acquiesce graciously, for it will be so. If you attempt to turn either father or Hotep-Re against me, you will regret it. As my wife you can be happy, treated with every consideration, but if you dare to attempt to thwart me in this, I shall make you very sorry. Remember well my sister, I shall be your lord and entitled to discipline you when and where I choose, and how I choose.'

He released her so suddenly that she stumbled and almost fell. She caught a last glimpse of his set face, his lips compressed in a tight line, then he turned from her and went his own way into the palace. She stood for a moment, striving to conquer her sobs. She could not come before her father in this state of emotional shock. She placed questioning fingers to ascertain if her robe had been torn or disarranged, then glanced down at her wrist where a bruise would soon form. Asenath was a royal princess and neither anger or fear could be allowed to show when servants and slaves would look on her, and she mastered herself in moments, and unhurriedly entered the palace and turned her steps to her father's apartments.

Pharaoh was seated at his writing table when she entered. He indicated silently that she was to seat herself, and continued to read the scroll in his hands.

She waited apprehensively for him to speak. When he did so, his words sent a cold chill through her body.

'It has been a long time, Asenath, since I have felt the temptation to take my chariot whip to your buttocks, but never have I felt it so strongly as last evening. Perhaps you will give me a reason for your boorish behaviour. I am quite at a loss to think of an adequate one.'

She looked up into his fierce face and her gaze did not falter. 'Forgive me, my lord father, it was inexcusable.'

'But why, Asenath — tell me why?'

'I do not know — I — I had a headache.'

'Headache or no — you know better than to make the family a hub of idle gossip.'

'My women had giggled about the girl. I was not pleased that Mern-ptah should offer her to me, after what I had heard. I was foolish to react in that way at the feast, I know it.'

'You accused your brother of sending the girl to spy on you. Whatever did you mean?'

She coloured and twisted her hands nervously in her lap. 'That — that was stupid — I — I don't know what I meant.' Then it came out in a rush. 'It's just that I do not seem to be able to escape the watchful eyes of people these days. Everyone seems to spy on me.'

'You are growing up, Asenath. All well-bred girls are chaperoned. Can you expect less — a royal princess?'

'No, my father.' Her answer was low.

'Serana and I have been concerned about you recently. You seem restless and ill-tempered. I understand this is part of growing up, but you must begin to think of your duties and less of your own wishes. You behaved like a shrewish fish wife. All Thebes must be discussing your tantrums.

55

This foolishness must cease.' He rose and went to the window. She waited in an agony of suspense for his decision about her fate. 'You will return to your apartments after this interview and remain there in seclusion for six days. Exercise you may take in the garden accompanied by Mem-net. During this time I would ask you to think seriously about your responsibilities as Throne Princess of The Two Lands. I do not wish to see you again until you have learned to conduct yourself as befits your station. You are fortunate that I have taken so lenient a view. You may go.'

She slipped to her knees to kiss his fingers and he turned, his mobile lips curving into a smile, despite the harshness of his tone. 'Go, kitten, and think on what I have said. I am distressed to see you unhappy, but I insist that you behave sensibly.'

'May I see my lady mother before I go to my apartments?'

He nodded and cupped her lovely chin in his hands. 'Of course, tell her your problems since you do not appear to be able to confide in me. She will visit you during your — imprisonment.' His voice lightly stressed the word annulling its severity. 'But nonetheless know that you are under the weight of my displeasure, and if you desire to redeem yourself, you will come to the next court function in a calmer frame of mind.'

As she reached the door he said quietly, 'Asenath, remember that we love you — all of us.'

She shook back the emotional tears which pricked at her lashes, bowed again and left his presence, to seek the solace of her stepmother's company.

When Mern-ptah presented himself at his father's request, Pharaoh was amused to see a frown creasing the brow of his elder son and a mutinous twist to the lips that boded trouble. Mindful of court etiquette the prince bowed as low as it was deemed necessary, but it was obvious he was in no mood for strictures. Suavely his father invited him to seat himself, then said mildly, 'I have interviewed Asenath, and seem to have got little sense from her. Do you not think I have some right to an explanation?'

Mern-ptah's frown darkened. 'My lord father her conduct puzzles me as much as you. I am at a loss to understand it.'

'There was gossip about you and the slave girl.'

'Oh that.' The prince rose and moved to the window, one hand on his hip. 'Yes that *is* possible.' He turned and the arrogant frown had changed now to a boyish flush of embarrassment.

'I confess I let most people think I had taken the girl for my pleasure, but I assure you, it was not so. Taia is but a child of

57

nine years old.'

'I see.' Not a muscle of Pharaoh's face moved, while he waited for his son to continue.

'Mardok offered me the girl as a new — experience.' He stressed the word ruefully. 'I was about to refuse when I saw how terrified she was.' He shrugged. 'She slept in my room, and I asked for her. I felt she would be happier with us and a suitable maid for Asenath. That is all there is to it, truly.'

Pharaoh relaxed and leaned back in his chair. 'So that was the way of it.'

'I cannot see why Asenath was so angry. Had the woman been favoured indeed by me, it would have made little difference. I did not consider Asenath jealous.'

'My son you have a great deal to learn about women — not least about the ones you marry.'

Mern-ptah turned directly to face him. 'Will you answer me one question directly, my father?'

'Certainly.'

'Will you give me Asenath as my wife?'

'Most assuredly — and with her the succession.'

'You have not had second thoughts — about Hotep-Re?'

Pharaoh shook his head. 'No, my son, *you*, not Hotep-Re, are the most fitted to

58

rule The Two Lands when I lie in my tomb. Hotep-Re knows that very well and, I am sure, is content.'

Mern-ptah came forward, his expression eager. 'Then will you order the marriage straight away? Asenath is sixteen. There can be no doubts about the matter then.'

'I will do so, as soon as I think the time is ripe.'

'Not at present?'

'I think Asenath unprepared. At the moment she is not ready to marry anyone. Tell me, have you quarrelled?'

Mern-ptah sighed. 'Yes, bitterly, but I was angry, it was but in the heat of the moment.'

Pharaoh tapped one hand on the table, then looked up at his son, his face thoughtful. 'I think I must send you away for a while.'

Angry colour flooded the prince's face. 'My lord, I have only recently returned to court. I looked for some time to relax and enjoy myself with the family. You are unjust, I was not at fault.'

Pharaoh's tone hardened. 'You question my decision?'

The prince checked and drew back. 'I have not that right, lord.'

'Indeed you have not. For a while it is best if you two do not meet. It will allow both of you time to consider your responsibilities to the other. Work is going badly at the new temple near the second cataract. Rehorem-heb is anxious to get the colossi into position during the cool season but the gateway is not complete. My commission tells me there are minor disturbances among the slaves. It is not convenient for me to leave Thebes at present. I propose to send you as my deputy. You have my leave to do what you think necessary to hasten the completion of the main building and to discipline both slaves and overseers, if you consider it salutary. I suggest you take the royal barge upstream tomorrow.'

Mern-ptah knew it was useless to argue. He bowed low and asked leave to depart. Pharaoh placed one hand on his shoulder and turned him to face his direct gaze. 'When you have completed what I ask, you may return immediately to Thebes. I trust you to handle this matter with competence.'

The prince moodily threw himself into a chair in his mother's room and reached for a fig from a small table at his side. Serana looked up from her embroidery, her lips curving into a smile at his resemblance to Ramoses. She made no comment but waited for him to air his grievance.

'My father sends me to take charge of work on the new temple,' he said briefly, wiping his fingers on a linen cloth. 'He thinks it better that I stay away from

Asenath for a while.' His black eyes swept her face interrogatively.

She nodded. 'There is wisdom in that.'

'He intends to announce my right to the succession soon, but feels she is not prepared yet for marriage.'

Serana put down her work and gazed at him, her eyes slightly puzzled. 'You do want Asenath as your wife?'

'Of course.'

'You will try to make her happy?'

'Certainly.' He rose and came to her, already contrite for his boorishness. 'My mother, do you doubt it?'

She took his hand and smiled up at him. 'I want you to try and understand her position. She has no choice in this matter . . . no, I know,' she checked him as he made to interrupt, 'neither have you, but in your case there are compensations. You may take other wives.'

'But she will be Great Royal Wife when the time comes, Queen of Egypt.'

'But will she have your love?'

He shrugged. 'She will have my . . . consideration.'

'For a woman that is not enough — believe me, I know. Your father is my whole life.'

He sat down on a stool by her side and peered up at her. 'You are trying to tell me that you are not always happy. You can be frank, I shall be discreet.'

'Of course I am happy, but I wasn't always so. You know I came to this land as a captive. I was very afraid of your father. I still am, but it does not prevent me from worshipping him. Unless you are wise, Asenath will live in dread of you. You do not wish this to be so?'

He laughed. 'I think it is a healthy omen for the marriage if the bride is somewhat in awe of her husband.'

'I am serious, my son.'

'And I, my mother. I know Asenath. If I do not rule her, she will attempt to dominate me. Already she has tried to subborn Hotep-Re. He has said nothing — but I know.'

Serana looked up startled and he leaned close to her. 'Marriage with Hotep-Re would mean that Asenath would rule Egypt. No, my mother, I intend that when the time comes, and may it be long if the Gods grant their favour, it shall be I alone who wield the flail. She may hold the crook if she wishes.'

Serana was silent for a moment, then he said quietly, 'I am glad she was not born of your body, my mother.'

'Marriage with a sister concerns you, my son?'

'No — but something Ptah Hoten once said disturbed me. Do not let it concern you. It is only that I wish Asenath to give me healthy children.'

She caught his hands and held them. 'I gave you life my son, but I love Asenath very dearly. I promised her mother I would guard her well. Swear to me that you will treat her with sympathy and patience. You will need it.'

'I love Asenath. Can I say more, but,' he laughed suddenly as he dropped a light kiss on her forehead, 'I shall not spare the whip if I feel it necessary. Do you deny me the right to discipline my wife?' His tone was light but he turned as she said nothing and looked into her eyes. 'My father — he did not . . .'

'A long time ago, my son, and for good reason.'

He was grave when he stood up to leave her. 'I will see you again this evening. I leave early in the morning. With luck and good fortune I will hasten the work, and return to your side before the Nile rises.'

5

Mern-ptah gazed disdainfully round the apartments which had been hastily set aside for his use. The building had been roughly constructed of mud brick, thatched for coolness, the open side curtained during the evening for privacy. Rabu and the chief engineer, a man of small wiry stature named Khufu, had used this building as an office and living quarters during the months they had been working on the new temple. They both hurriedly collected their belongings and moved out to make room for their exalted guest. Inside, despite its rough construction, the apartment was pleasing enough. A small room had been curtained off as a sleeping chamber, and the large outer room held work tables, chests and several plain but comfortable chairs. The prince indicated to the bearers where they were to place his chests of personal belongings and sank down into a chair near to the work bench and idly picked up the plans.

'You need have no fear, gentlemen. I am here merely to speed up work schedules. I know nothing whatever about construction problems which I shall leave entirely in your hands. I am concerned that we are behind with the plans. The reasons for this we must discuss in some detail. However it is good of you to vacate your quarters. I regret the inconvenience.'

Rabu bowed respectfully. 'My lord, it is no trouble. There are several huts we can use for our work, and we are out of doors most of the day.'

'How long does my Lord Prince intend to stay?' Khufu asked, toying nervously with a pair of measuring dividers.

'I intend to remain until the work is completed,' the prince said curtly, 'and since I wish to return to the comforts of Thebes as soon as possible, I am as anxious as you are to speed up the process.'

'My lord has brought attendants?' Rabu enquired respectfully.

'No, I came immediately. I supposed you could find me slaves to work in the apartments.'

'At once, lord. It will be an honour to provide for you.'

Mern-ptah undid the heavy gold pectoral which was chafing his neck and laid it down on the table. 'My needs are few. I am used to campaigning. You will not need to fuss over me. You can leave me. Send a slave with refreshment and water. Later, gentlemen, when I am bathed and rested, it would give me pleasure if you would both dine here with me.'

Murmuring polite words of acceptance, they withdrew.

Mern-ptah had spent the previous evening with his mother and later had had a short discussion with his younger brother. Hotep-Re had shown concern over the quarrel with Asenath. Mern-ptah's anger at his enforced exile from the court was made plain, and he had attempted to pour oil on troubled waters without success however.

Never disturbed by any day-time irritations, Mern-ptah had slept soundly and embarked as ordered, early the next day. His mother and father had formally bidden him 'god-speed'. Of Asenath, he had seen no sign. The journey had been short but irksome, and now that he had arrived, he could see that much work still remained to be done. The façade of the outer pylon was incomplete and the pavement not even begun. The heat was intolerable and he turned into the sleeping chamber to wait until a slave arrived with water for bathing.

The thin young man who eventually presented himself was undoubtedly of Semite origin. His thick curly hair hung low on his brow and his nose was overlong and hooked. Mern-ptah judged him to be slightly younger than himself. His Egyptian was faultless, so he had probably been born in slavery, though his attitude was not one of servile devotion. When ordered, he placed down the earthen jar and bowed low, but his large dark eyes flickered over the length of the prince's figure in a glance of frank curiosity.

'I will stand over here on this shallow trough. Come, pour water over my body and hand me a towel.' The slave obeyed and enveloped Mern-ptah in the clean coarse linen.

The prince indicated a fresh kilt, which lay folded ready on the bed and re-clothed himself, then pushed his feet into comfortable reed sandals.

'Your name?' he asked, as the slave made no motion to leave him.

'Yussef, lord.'

'What is your work here?'

The slave shrugged. 'I serve in various ways; thatching the roofs of the huts, making mortar, occasionally waiting on the overseers. I am not skilled in the cutting of stone.'

'You will do well enough to serve me when I need it. You may tell Rabu. You can go.'

Again Mern-ptah was struck by the lack of servility in the slave's attitude. He bowed low enough, but he showed no sign that he was awed by the honour of serving the future lord of The Two Lands. Mern-ptah turned away piqued, then promptly forgot the slave.

Dinner was a surprisingly pleasant meal. He found he was hungry, after the river journey and the two officials made refreshing companions. They had been long away from court and they listened with interest to his account of the recent rebellion in Kush, and to news of the court officials they numbered among their acquaintances. His eyes fell on the young Hebrew slave-girl who helped to serve them, and when she was left alone to stand waiting with the jars of wine in case of need, his bold eyes swept her slim figure. She appeared to not notice his scrutiny, and when Rabu and Khufu rose to take their departure since it was late and they professed their intentions of making a very early start to work the following day, he smilingly dismissed them and as the girl too, prostrated herself and asked in a low voice if he required anything further, he motioned to her to stand and drew her closer. She shrank back, alarmed at his touch and he reached up and put back her head veil, revealing her long black hair, rippling to the waist.

'You are very pretty. What is your name?' His voice was pleasant. His ill humour had disappeared under the relaxing charm of good food and wine. He was in the mood for dalliance, and was unprepared for the girl's terrified reaction.

'I am called Ruth. My brother Yussef served you earlier.'

'Indeed, I remember the slave — yes, you resemble each other. You have been long here?'

'Yes, lord.' She tried to draw back but his grip was like steel on her thin wrist.

'Do not be afraid of me. What troubles you?'

'If my lord has everything he wishes, I will leave.' Again she made an attempt to withdraw from his clasp.

'And you wish to leave? You do not find me attractive?'

'My lord — I beg of you.'

He let go one arm and tilted up her chin, ignoring her vain struggles. Now thoroughly alarmed, she beat up at him with her free hand, and he drew back, a regal frown darkening his brow. He was not used to such treatment. He desired to honour the girl, and she was attempting to repulse him.

'My lord . . . my brother will be angry, please . . . please allow me to go.' Her distress was pathetic.

Intoxicated by the wine and already irritated by the day's events, he was angrier than such an encounter merited. At court any woman would have known better than to misunderstand his advances, or been more skilfully able to counter them, but this girl had no such experience. She backed from him until she stumbled over an open chest and slipped to her knees, then falling forward, she threw out her hands in supplication and sobbed out a plea to him to allow her to go.

Angrily he pulled her to her feet and crushed her against his body once more, then abruptly, disgusted by her tears, pushed her as quickly away. At that moment, Rabu called respectfully and asked if he might enter. Mern-ptah answered curtly, giving permission, and the girl, still weeping, turned away. The overseer took in the situation at a glance and angrily looked from the sulky prince to the distressed girl.

'My lord, if she has angered you, I will have her flogged.'

'It is nothing. I am gone in wine, friend. The girl may leave.'

Ruth ran from the hut and Mern-ptah turned back to Rabu. 'Do you wish to see me about something?'

'No, my lord.'

'But you returned . . .'

'Oh.' The man recollected himself hurriedly. 'Forgive me, I left one of the plans. We would like to consult it before the morning. Ah, here it is. Have I your leave to go?'

Mern-ptah had already poured himself another goblet of wine. He turned and swayed. The potent liquid had left him with a warm comfortable glow. He nodded smiling and the overseer withdrew.

It was rarely that he imbibed too freely and he discovered his mistake when he opened his eyes the following day. The slave, Yussef, stood by his bed with a pitcher. He had opened the door and the sun's glare was an agony. Mern-ptah hastily closed his eyes and gestured arrogantly to the door.

'Fool, shut out the light. Put the pitcher down.'

'Forgive me, lord.' The slave's eyes flickered almost contemptuously over him as he sat up in the grateful shade and held his aching head in his hands. 'Rabu said you wished to see the work begin early and requested that I should wake you.'

'True.' Mern-ptah pointed to the goblet near his bed. 'Give me some water.' He drank thirstily and after a moment, stood up. The movement was not wise. He experienced immediate sensations of distinct unbalance and acute nausea. The slave brought a bowl to the bed. His voice was respectful but cool. 'I should sit down, lord. You will feel better if you vomit.' The prince looked up at him angrily, and winced at the sudden pain the sharp movement caused. He could not recollect ever having felt so wretched. He retched miserably and gave way to the weakness of the moment. The slave was efficient and skilful. Afterwards he bathed his face and persuaded him to lie back with a napkin soaked in cold water over his aching temples. Half an hour later, he was able to struggle up, feeling half himself and ungrateful enough to be irritated that the slave had seen him at a disadvantage. He curtly dismissed him and slowly splashed water over himself and dressed. He was vaguely embarrassed and ashamed. Anxious to begin to see for himself why the delays were occurring, he donned a striped headdress to protect himself from the sun's rays, and pushed aside the curtained partition of his apartment.

The scene was one of activity, busy enough to satisfy the demands of the hardest of taskmasters. Heavy limestone blocks, which were to form the façade of the temple, were being prepared to the left of the huts. Slaves were smoothing the top surface, while the corners were being skilfully shaped by the stone-cutters. One large block was being pulled slowly up the wood and brick ramp to its position. Mern-ptah counted approximately sixty or seventy male slaves pulling on the ropes, while several young women ran alongside pouring water to prevent friction on the rollers. Rabu was consulting with Khufu and they acknowledged his presence with low bows. Slapping an ornamental fly whisk against his thigh, he came over to them, screwing his eyes against the glare, hoping the ravages of the previous night's carousing were not still apparent.

'The slaves appear to be doing well now,' he said coolly, accepting their greeting with a gracious nod, 'so why are we behind schedule?'

Rabu cleared his throat nervously. 'My lord, the heat has been excessive this season, which means that we cannot overwork the slaves during the noon hours. When the Nile rises, it will be cooler and we can proceed more quickly, also food-stocks are low. We were waiting for fresh supplies to be delivered, but the Nile traffic is poor at this time. Slaves cannot do heavy work without food.'

'True.' Mern-ptah shaded his eyes and watched as a young man withdrew himself from a group of stone-cutters and moved over to another. He paused as he saw the heads of the men at work on the stone draw close together, as if in consultation. He frowned. 'I heard tell of subversion on the site. Would you say there was any truth in that?' He turned sharply and confronted the two officials.

Rabu shrugged. 'My lord there are always a few slaves who will talk of rebellion. It rarely comes to anything.'

'You have punished the offenders?'

73

'It is difficult to pick out the rebels. If I see a slave slacking, I order him flogged, but as Your Royal Father knows well, I have always considered it advantageous to handle the slaves without recourse to the whip, whenever possible. I have always found my methods effective.'

'But not this time apparently.' The prince turned back to his survey of the site.

'My lord,' Khufu's voice was dry, 'I assure you, no problems beset the project other than the usual ones. The second the heat dies down, work will return to normal, and we shall speed up.'

'And Rehoremheb's work on the statues will be impeded.'

'With luck we will make up the time.'

'I am here to see that we *do,* with or without luck. Call two of your men here. I will not keep them long.'

Mern-ptah moved away and Khufu sighed. Work had been hard but peaceable until the young prince came. Both men could see trouble ahead and feared the outcome. Rabu had made light of the matter, but indeed the temper of the slaves had run high, sparked off by the poor food and irritation of the additional heat. Try as he might, he had been unable to alleviate their working conditions. If the prince interfered and made their lot harder to bear, he feared they would become openly rebellious.

The two overseers approached the prince with awe and threw themselves down in the dust at his feet. He moved one hand, indicating that the two men were to stand and pointed to where timber balks were being cut and prepared for use under the ramps.

'Cut me a sturdy stake, sharpen it well and embed it deep in sand and mortar, there, near the pylon entrance, where it will be well in evidence.' Then as the two gazed at him wonderingly, he turned away and spoke over his shoulder, 'The sharpened end uppermost, naturally.'

One of the men shrugged, while the older one looked uneasily after the retreating prince, then without exchanging a word they settled to the appointed task.

Mern-ptah was in no good humour over the mid-day break. The two officials, sensing his mood, said little either. He drank sparingly and pushed away the proffered food which the slave-girl timidly served to them. His temples still throbbed abominably and he felt sick and the smell of the rich dishes nauseated him further. The heat was at its most oppressive, and he longed to retire to the shade of the sleeping apartment and rest, but he wished to speak to the slaves before they began their labours again, and obviously after the meal would be the most convenient time. He indicated his wishes to Rabu, who dispatched a task-master to call them together near the uncompleted gateway.

Even Khufu wiped the heat from his sweating face and shoulders, while they stood in the unrelenting heat of the mid-day. The slaves lay flat on their faces when Rabu so ordered them to prostrate themselves before the Prince of The Two Lands. Mern-ptah disdained even to toss his head against the insistent buzz of a blow-fly. He instructed Rabu to order them to lift their heads and give him their attention.

'You may wonder why I have been sent here,' he said at last, coldly. 'I am here because the work is behind schedule. I have been offered many excuses.' He paused as a little murmur went through the community. 'But I refuse to listen to any more. The work must proceed more quickly. It has come to my attention that there are signs of dissatisfaction and talk of rebellion. These will cease.' Again he paused and they waited sullenly. 'You are aware that no one may utter a death sentence without the confirmation of Pharaoh except by the word of his chosen deputy. I am so.' He turned so that their eyes were drawn to the sharp-ened stake. 'I will impale any slave who is guilty of speaking one word of dissention or any man, woman or child who disobeys the overseers. I hope I have made myself clear. There will be no appeal. I have spoken. I shall be obeyed. Go now, resume work, let me not have to prove my threat.' He did not wait to see what effect his words had. He turned and walking with easy, graceful strides, re-entered his own apartments.

When Ruth brought water to her brother, he drank thirstily from the goatskin bottle, then as she moved to go, he detained her.

'One moment. Do you wait on table at the royal apartment, tonight?'

She nodded, then lowered her eyes.

'You will be discreet, my sister.'

She turned away and made no answer, then he put out a hand, and turned her by the chin, to look at him.

'I mean it. You must promise. He means what he says.'

Frightened, she stared back at him, then nodded and moved away. An old man who was assisting Yussef in the mixing of the mortar, stood up and gazed after her.

'She is a rare pretty lass,' he said, 'and she has eyes for no one save Reuben.'

'I wish she had a plainer face, old one,' Yussef said grimly.

'She has taken his eye then? I am not surprised.'

'So far she has remained unmolested, but I fear for her, if she repulses him.'

'It is not a pretty death.' The old man's eyes moved uneasily to where the sharpened stake stood starkly upright against the unfinished gateway. 'I remember once . . .'

'Tell us, Simeon.' A strong bass voice sounded behind them, and Yussef greeted the newcomer with a smile.

'You are too late by moments, Reuben. She has just left.'

The big slave smiled back and rubbed the sweat from his eyes. 'Aye, I know, I begged a drink of her on the way up. We shall soon need more mortar. I made it an excuse to pause for a moment. My back is near breaking. You were saying Simeon — you remember an execution?'

The old man nodded uneasily. 'We will be wise to act carefully and keep close mouths. Such a death is unthinkable.'

Reuben's usually merry brown eyes were grave. 'You are right, old man. I think some of our friends have been criminally foolish. It will not be good to anger *that* one.'

Yussef's comment was short. 'He seemed to me little more than a spoilt boy.'

'Man enough to condemn you to a lingering death.' Reuben's answer was equally brief.

'Lingering indeed.' Simeon put down the trowel, his lined face working with emotion. 'It must be nigh on twenty years ago since I saw a man impaled. He struck an overseer who lashed him. He was my friend. The young prince's father was here on a visit. He had not then ascended the throne. Very like him, he was. I only saw him the once.' He fell silent and the other two made no move to hurry him. They knew the ways of old men. 'Four days it took him to die — aye.' He lifted his eyes to those of Yussef. 'See that she is sensible lad, nothing is worth that, nothing in this world, or the next these Egyptians speak of. You can take the mortar now. It is finished.'

Reuben watched, as the old man moved off and he laid one hand on his friend's forearm. 'Tell her, her safety is all that matters to me.'

Yussef nodded, then the other lifted the board with the prepared mortar and returned to the site.

At the end of the working day, Yussef sought out Khefren the healer priest. It was his custom to assist the priest to prepare his small hut for the following day.

'Yussef, you work hard all through the day. That is enough,' Khefren said gravely.

'I do not call this work, priest,' Yussef said lightly, as he glanced round for any service he could render. 'I find pleasure in watching you work whenever I can. It holds a great fascination for me.'

'You are not sickened by the sight of blood and crushed flesh?'

'No, priest, only when it is shed wilfully

by the order of a man in authority.'

The priest glanced at him shrewdly, under his shaven eyebrows.

'I heard of the prince's declaration, though I was not present.'

'I will not talk reason, priest, but I merely say I wonder at a man's right to so glibly talk of taking the life from another.'

The priest lowered his eyes. 'The teaching in the Temple of Ptah is one of mercy and forbearance.'

'And yet I understand that Pharaoh is a worshipper of Ptah.'

'That is true. The prince's attitude is surprising, but he is in charge, it is not for me to question. He is the son of the gods.'

Yussef was silent and Khefren saw a faint smile play about the lips of the slave. He decided to ignore it and turn their discussion to other matters.

'When work is completed on this temple, I will ask Rabu if he will release you for service part of the time, assisting me. At the moment, I know he is hard pushed to find labour, skilled or unskilled, and he would probably refuse. I think it wiser to wait for a more auspicious moment.'

Yussef's cheeks flushed with pleasure. 'You would truly teach me some of your art?'

'Yes, I feel you would be an apt pupil. Had you been free, you might have made a skilled physician, but I can teach you only the rudiments. The priests at the temple are skilled surgeons. Yet I can do a great deal here to fight minor sicknesses and treat injuries. You can assist me to treat disorders of the bowels and fevers, sicknesses most common among the workers, and dress the minor wounds. You must learn hygiene and take special care over your personal cleanliness. Watch your hands. A healer's hands must be sensitive and as smooth as possible.' He smiled. 'Be patient, Yussef, once the hard work on this pylon is finished, Rabu will release you. He is an understanding man and knows your worth. In the meantime, guard your temper.'

Yussef turned hastily. 'You wrong me, master. I am no hot-head.'

'Not until you are roused.'

The slave flushed darkly and nodded. 'I am more easily roused in defence of another,' he said briefly and saluting the priest, courteously withdrew.

As the days passed, work progressed on the façade of the temple, no respite came from the intense heat and the slaves suffered under the pressure of the taskmasters, who were nervously aware of the frowning attention of the young prince, who seemed to be everywhere on the site, watching, and questioning. The supply boats did not arrive and Rabu prayed the gods for some let-up which would ease conditions. Once over his weakness after the first night's carousel, Mern-ptah seemed untiring and completely unaffected by the heat. He showed an intelligent interest in the plans and had he been less irritating in his demands, the two officials would have found him a rewarding pupil. It was clear they would have no fool for their future Pharaoh — and no easy master either. In their turn they put pressure to bear on their underlings, who passed it on to the sweating slaves. Temporarily the work seemed to have speeded up, but Rabu feared they could not continue long under those conditions at that rate.

He was consulting with Khufu one morning, several days later, when he was aware of voices raised in argument. Hurriedly the two men hastened to the scene of the disturbance. An overseer was hotly disputing with two of his slaves. His whip was raised to strike and Rabu noticed, surprised, that the two insurgents seemed to be Reuben and Yussef, neither of whom had shown, in the past, any tendency towards conduct of a rebellious nature. Even from that distance, Reuben's voice carried.

'You know well enough, Yussef is no stone-cutter. He is unskilled and liable to injury. Call one of the other slaves.'

The overseer's angry retort was not audible, but it was clear that he was in a mood to brook no interference and Rabu could see him gesticulating towards a huge block of stone standing on end, which was apparently too large and needed splitting.

A cool voice broke into the argument.

'Is the slave rebellious? Order him to obey, or arrest him and keep him close for the punishment decreed.' Mern-ptah was also in no mood to brook defiance, and signalled for the overseer to use his whip, if need be, to compel obedience.

'You can't do that,' Reuben's shocked notes cried out over the sound of hammering. 'Yussef helps the healer priest. He must not make his hands calloused. He works hard enough at his own jobs. Be reasonable.'

Rabu was reluctant to interfere, as the prince had already spoken, and drew back a little uncertain how to proceed. He knew the slave Yussef, and was anxious not to bring harm to the boy, who had his uses and was trustworthy, although not skilled in the cutting of stone. He judged it best to allow the overseer to assert his authority at the moment, while later he would relieve the slave. He shrugged eloquently and turning his back, prepared to retire to the office with the engineer, to continue their discussion. The voices appeared to have died down. Doubtless the incident would soon be forgotten. He hoped so. He had regard for both the young slaves.

A sudden crash and a warning scream, hurriedly echoed by other voices, made him turn. Horror-stricken, he stood for a second, rooted to the ground, then galvanised his muscles into sudden action and ran forward, Khufu blundering along behind. The huge stone had rocked in its position; something had jarred it, possibly Reuben had clumsily caught it when stepping back to avoid the overseer's whip. He was now trapped under the heavy weight of the stone. Fast as Rabu was, the prince was swifter. He leapt down from the rise, where he was watching the argument and grim-lipped, knelt by the trapped slave. He was unprepared for the action of the young Semite, Yussef. With an infuriated snarl, he sprang at the kneeling prince, his mallet lifted to strike.

'You are responsible,' he shouted. 'Without your interference Reuben would not have been hurt. You shall not injure any more of us.' The rest of the tirade was lost, as two of the guards pulled him back. The mallet fell harmlessly some yards from Mern-ptah, who did not even flinch, but gestured to the guards to withdraw the slave. Fighting and screaming with fury and grief, he was dragged away.

Rabu knelt by the prince's side, noting that Reuben seemed unconscious fortunately. His right leg and hip and the right side of his body were trapped beneath the stone. Blood oozed from one side of his mouth. After the first scream, he had made no sound. A guard looked down dispassionately, and drew his dagger.

'Best to end it, lord,' he said crisply. 'We can do nothing for him. If you will retire, I will deal with the matter.'

'Fool, no.' Mern-ptah spat at him and knocked the dagger from his hand. 'Wait, where is the healer priest?'

A little knot of murmuring slaves drew back as the shaven-headed priest of Ptah approached and mutely requesting permission, bent over the injured slave. He bent his ear to the left side of the body, which was clear of the stone, and lifted back the eye-lid of one eye.

'Does he live, priest?' The prince's question was harsh.

'Yes, lord, but it is difficult to say how badly he is injured.'

'Will we harm him further if we attempt to lift the stone?'

'It is a difficult operation but must be done at once. At the moment his Ka has left his body. He feels no pain. It is best to make the attempt now. I can then examine him further.'

Mern-ptah rose and questioned Khufu. 'What is best to be done? It must be done with care.'

The engineer pursed his lips and gravely shook his head. 'We need timber stakes for levers. Give me the use of ten men and I think it can be done.'

'Take those you need and do your best, but watch for danger. We can ill afford to risk any further accidents.' He looked down once more at the pale-faced slave, then turned away and left the task to those better fitted to the leverage, which would free him. Rabu said quietly, 'It was an accident, lord, do not blame yourself.'

'The Semite was right. Had I not interfered, it would not have happened. You know the man?'

'Yes, he is a skilled worker — and conscientious.'

'Worse still then. You think there is a chance he will recover?'

'It is hard to tell, lord. If he is crushed . . .'

'Quite so,' Mern-ptah sighed, then frowned as the young captain in command of the guards approached and gave the royal salute. 'Well, what is it?' he questioned sharply.

'The other slave, my lord, he who attacked you, shall we dispatch him instantly, or do you wish him impaled as an example to the rest?'

Mern-ptah checked and stared into the officer's stony countenance, then looked away.

'No, no,' he said, then a little uncertainly, 'I do not think it necessary for such a harsh lesson. The boy was distraught. Have him well flogged, then release him.'

'My lord, he sought your life.'

'He believed I had taken that of his friend. Obey me please. I know what I am doing.'

The captain hesitated, well knowing the danger he would be in if news of the affair reached the ears of Pharaoh, his first duty obviously being to protect the Royal Heir apparent, but the prince's tone was haughty, and he saluted once again, and obediently withdrew.

Mern-ptah stood watching anxiously, as the men heaved on the wooden timber balks at the careful instruction of Kihufu. The engineer looked up and called across to the prince.

'He is free, my lord.'

Mern-ptah slowly walked over to the spot where the healer priest was kneeling by the injured slave. He stood silent, while he waited for the verdict. When the priest rose his expression was grave.

'The hip is broken and possibly the ankle. There appears to be no bone crushed — but

I cannot tell the extent of the internal injuries. Blood from the mouth gives indications that they are extensive.'

'Then he will die?'

The priest hesitated. 'Most likely, lord, unless . . .'

'Can you not help him?'

'No lord, I am no skilled surgeon. Ptah Hoten perhaps, even then it is possible his injuries will prove fatal.'

'You think if he were taken to the Temple of Ptah in Thebes, there is a chance that he might survive.'

'It is possible, lord, if the slave has a strong constitution, but how could we take him? To carry him in a chariot would kill him. The journey to fetch a priest and return, would take too long. I am afraid — I can give him seeds of the poppy to ease the pain. It is all we can do.'

'No.' The prince shook his head. 'We will go by river.'

'My lord, we have no boat here till the supply boats come,' Rabu reminded him quietly of the facts.

'There are no boats at the nearest village? A small craft — a fisherman's?'

'One of the men has such a boat but he never ventures far from the village. He is an old man and I do not think we could trust him to go as far as Thebes. He would be afraid to enter the temple.'

88

'No, that is not necessary. I will go.'

'*You,* my lord,' Rabu's voice expressed his incredulity.

Mern-ptah smiled, a sudden gleam shining out from the fierce countenance, and irradiating it. 'You live no confidence in me, Rabu? I am a skilled sailor. I can easily manage a light craft.' His lips twisted wryly. 'It appears that I am the one person who can be most easily spared. No.' He put a hand on the other's arm as he moved to expostulate. 'You know this is so. If there is a chance to save the boy, then I must go. Send to the village and tell the fisherman to bring his boat to this landing stage. You had better buy the boat. Pay him generously.'

Rabu made one half-hearted attempt to prevent what he thought to be a foolish action. 'My lord, the craft will be filthy and possibly in poor condition.'

'True old friend, but I am a skilled navigator and strong swimmer.' He clapped the official on the back. 'I have been overturned many times while wildfowling with my brother. I can manage.'

He looked across to the healer's hut where the slaves had carried Reuben.

'The priest will do what he can for him to prepare him for the journey. I will change and pack what I need. See that food and water are assembled on the landing stage.'

The two officials, bewildered but defeated, hustled the overseers about the business of preparation.

Later, when the prince presented himself in the healer's hut, he found the slave still unconscious but strapped tightly to a timber board. The priest gave a quick admiring glance at Mern-ptah's attire. He had chosen a brief coarse loin-cloth and striped head-dress. This, and the cloak thrown over one shoulder, would give him some protection from the glare of the sun on the vulnerable parts of his body and from the chill of the desert night. He had stripped himself of all jewelry, which would weigh him down if he were forced to swim and irritate while he handled the paddles to steer. A sturdy knife was pushed into his loin-cloth and he wore plain reed sandals.

'How is he?'

'There is no change in his condition, lord. I have strapped him so that he will not be jolted. It is imperative he should be kept as still as possible. I have packed a phial of drug which you may force between his lips if he appears to be in severe pain. On no account are you to feed him, nor even to give him water, no matter how pitifully he pleads for it. Do you understand?'

'Perfectly. I will obey you. Until he is under the care of Ptah Hoten, I will give him nothing.'

'I have prepared oils for you to massage into your cramped muscles and to protect you from burning.'

'Good.'

'May Ptah protect you and heal the slave.'

'I will not neglect to pray, priest, I promise you. Have the slave carefully conveyed to the landing stage.'

Rabu walked quickly up, as the injured man was carried out. 'My lord,' he said anxiously, 'will you manage alone? The boat is ready. It is very small, but can you manage the injured man?'

'I have thought of that.' Mern-ptah frowned as his black eyes surveyed the flimsy craft into which the slaves were packing necessities. It was leaking already. It would take all of his skill to convey it downstream safely. 'No. I shall need one man to bale out when necessary and keep an eye on the slave. I shall take Master Interference, over there. Cut him down from the whipping post. He will do.'

Rabu's face betrayed his horror.

'My lord, he attempted to kill you.'

'For the sake of his friend. If he wishes to save him, he will do his best for him and for me. Do as I say, man. Send him here to me. I want no delays.'

The overseer bowed low and moved off to obey. He had always found the prince's father unpredictable, but the boy's behav-

iour today was altogether beyond his com-
prehension, but it was plain that he must
be obeyed. He would spend every free moment during the next few days petitioning
the gods for their protection, for if any harm
came to the Royal Heir, it would be better
for him to take his own life, rather than to
face the wrath of Pharaoh.

6

Yussef eased himself in his bonds, while keeping his eyes tightly shut against the sun's glare. The pain of the flogging had been considerable; he could still feel the rawness of the open wounds. Had he thought about the gravity of his position, it would have sent him sick with horror. He had made an attempt on the life of the divine person of the Heir to The Two Lands. This was but a foretaste and his death which would follow, would be neither quick nor clean; but Yussef's thoughts concerned not his own approaching fate, but Reuben's. The agony of his loss enveloped his mind in black despair and left no place for even fear. He knew well that the guards would swiftly dispatch the big man with the booming laugh, who was his own dearest companion and his sister's most ardent wooer. Common sense told him it was the kindest action, but even his concern about his sister could not break into the bitterness of mourning. He made no move to resist when he felt himself released from the leathern thongs which secured his wrists to the rings of the whipping post, and allowed his nerveless weight to fall on to the sand. His most crying need was for water, but it seemed that even this was to be denied him, for the guard officer ordered him harshly to his feet.

'Get up. Bow your head and face the prince.'

Yussef fought back the nausea which threatened to unman him before his tormenters, and head lowered mechanically rubbed his numbed wrists.

'Pick up that cloak at your feet, and come with me. You can walk?'

Yussef nodded and moved forward obediently. It seemed an odd request. Surely the guards would drag him to the impalement stake, but it was better to walk manfully. The prince had already haughtily stalked away when he lifted his head.

Rabu bent and picked up the cloak which the prince had thrown at the boy's feet. He knew Yussef was weak with pain and the effort of stooping would be disastrous.

'Here, lad, tie on this headcloth, you will need it. Come to the landing stage.'

Yussef limped to the water's edge, and still dazed, stared down into the boat. A sob broke from his lips at the sight of his friend's body tied to the board. The prince's voice broke across his amazement.

'Come, we have no time to waste. Every moment lessens your friend's chances of recovery. We take him downriver to Thebes. Can you handle a boat?'

'No, my lord.'

The prince sighed. 'As I feared, nevertheless you can bale out the water and take care of Reuben. Get in, step lightly or you'll overturn us. Rabu, I will take my leave. I trust you now to press on with the work. I will return with the next supply boat to leave Thebes.'

'May the gods guard you well.'

'They will do so. Am I not their son?' He laughed at the embarrassed silence which met his words. The officials had a vague sense that he was making fun of them, then he pushed off into midstream and was forced to give all his attention to the frail craft. He did not even see their anxious eyes follow the three out of sight round a bend in the river bank.

Yussef dare not move about in the boat. His eyes were fixed on the pale face of his friend. The prince's harsh voice lashed him into action.

'Bale out, fool. We are already shipping water. Keep busy or none of us will make it to Thebes.'

Obediently Yussef picked up an earthen bowl and began to empty the water which had collected in the bottom of the vessel, overside.

'The priest says your friend is injured internally and needs the attention of the skilled healer priest of Ptah. We must give him nothing until we reach the Temple; no water, not a drop, only the phial of liquid to ease his pain, there in the linen satchel. He may wake and beg for water. You are to take no heed of his ravings. You may bathe his face, but nothing else. You hear me?'

'Yes, lord.' Yussef continued with his baling and after some minutes the level went down and he was able to rest. He watched, his eyes respectfully lowered, while the prince steered competently a course which kept them far enough from the bank to give no problems of shallow water, and allowed the current to carry them downstream. The sun beat down on their unprotected bodies, but it would soon become cooler and Yussef, used to working in the full glare, ignored the discomfort and allowed his eyes to scan the banks.

He could see the peasants toiling at the irrigation channels, the donkeys patiently moving the wheels which lifted buckets of water to the surface to be poured out over the thirsty fields. Soon the Nile god would flood the banks and make thick black fertile mud of the parched earth. Once or twice a crocodile lazily slithered into the water.

When it was too dark to safely proceed, they tied up on the western bank and the prince climbed on to the shore. He ate and drank and ordered Yussef to take refreshment. The slave drank thirstily and eyed his friend with pity. He sat still when ordered, while Mern-ptah roughly but efficiently smoothed an aromatic salve into the open wounds on his back. He caught his breath sharply to avoid giving the little gasps of pain he was determined not to divulge. The strong smelling ointment would serve a double purpose of keeping off insect irritation, and once over the ordeal, he was glad of the relief it gave him.

Mern-ptah rolled himself in his cloak, and bade him keep watch by Reuben until he awoke. They were some way off from any village and the night was chill. He was glad of the warmth of the cloak which had been thrown to him. He kept Reuben well covered and watched anxiously for any change in his friend's condition. The sounds of night were intensified by the quietness and he jumped at bird calls and the dismal croaking of frogs some way off.

A moan riveted his attention immediately, and he bent his ear to his friend's lips. The eyes had flickered open and Reuben tried unsuccessfully to move and finding himself pinioned, gazed blankly up at Yussef.

'Lie still, my friend. You must not attempt

to move. You are gravely hurt.'

'What happened?' The voice was very weak.

'The stone fell and trapped you. We take you to Thebes for tending. Try to rest now.'

'Give me water, Yussef, I beg of you.'

Yussef turned away, dreading to give the answer. 'That I cannot do, my friend. The priest says we must give you nothing yet. I will moisten your lips and bathe your face.'

'I am fevered.'

'I know, but you must be quiet. Is the pain bad? I have a drug which will help if you need it.'

'No — I think not . . .' He lay still while Yussef wiped his sweat-streaked face and licked pathetically at the moistened lips. Yussef steeled himself to resist further pleading for water, but Reuben made no more efforts to persuade him.

'What have they done to you? Your back is raw.' The voice was a little stronger now and Yussef made a slight embarrassed laugh.

'It is nothing — a punishment well deserved. I threatened the prince with my mallet.'

'You did what?'

'Be not afraid. I missed him. He sleeps soundly over there.'

'He spared your life?'

'I find it difficult to understand myself, do

not let it worry you. His purposes will be made plainer in Thebes.'

As if too wearied to even think further, Reuben's eyes closed and Yussef eased his cramped muscles and replaced the top on the water jar. Apparently his friend was not in enough pain to prevent him resting, and that was a relief to know.

Some hours later he felt his shoulder touched and Mern-ptah bade him get some sleep. 'Lie down now until dawn. I will watch the slave. Has he recovered consciousness?'

'Yes, lord, for a few moments, but he drifted off again. I offered him the drug, but he refused it.'

'Just so, I will administer it if he wakes.'

Yussef lay down, wrapped in his cloak, and worn out by anxiety, pain and exposure, was soon asleep.

He was awakened by a rough shake and hurriedly sat upright at once. The prince pointed to the food supplies and kicked off his sandals.

'Eat and prepare for the journey. I intend to swim. When I return, we must be ready. I intend to travel far before Ra rises into the sky. Hurry now.'

Yussef watched him dive into the river and swim strongly upstream. He gave his attention to Reuben, who looked wan and pale by the early light of dawn, but appeared to be sleeping soundly. He lifted the phial of drug and saw a third of it gone. So the prince had administered it, while he was sleeping. Although the food was of the best, and better by far than that he normally received in the slaves' huts, he hardly tasted it, but was glad of the water. Immediately afterwards, he stripped and splashed water on his body, then redressed and packed the equipment ready for the journey. Almost at once, the prince pulled himself on-shore, shook himself, then wrang out his prince's lock and without a word, re-donned his linen kilt and belt. He flung the sandals into the boat and indicated his readiness to proceed.

The journey through the morning was uneventful and no words were passed. Once or twice Reuben moaned and Yussef did what he could to ease his suffering. When the heat became unbearable, they pulled into the bank and slept for two hours under the shade of the papyrus which grew tall and thick. The second the glare lessened, Mern-ptah was eager to continue. He judged that despite the sluggishness of the current, they could reach Thebes by the evening. The boat shipped water again and Yussef's arms ached with the continual baling out that was required to keep them afloat.

Towards dusk, they almost encountered

disaster. Three hippotami splashed and lumbered in the water ahead of them. One glance at the unwieldy brutes and Mernptah frowned and steered for the shore.

'We must heave to for a while.'

'My lord it is already dusk. If we push on, we might arrive before sun-down.'

'Not if those brutes overset the boat. The animals are harmless but would be disastrous if they came too close. We must wait.'

In a fever of impatience, the two men watched the ugly but oddly fascinating creatures sporting in the thick ooze of the river shallows. The prince watched the sky. Already the red blood haze was disappearing. Night would soon fall quickly and he had hoped to reach the Temple before then. A choking cough brought his attention to their charge. Yussef bent over him and looked up worriedly, as a thin trickle of blood oozed from the corner of Reuben's mouth.

The internal bleeding had started again. The prince steeled his heart against the husky half-delirious pleas for water.

'Give him the rest of the drug in the phial. We may be delayed some time. It will give some relief,' he said quietly.

Yussef obeyed and lifted Reuben's head to force the liquid between his teeth which were gritted against the pain.

'I think relief is of little use now, lord,' he

replied as calmly. 'Time is the main factor. If we fail to reach Thebes tonight, we shall carry a dead man with us.'

Mern-ptah frowned and peered across the wide expanse of water. 'So far I have avoided the strong current near the centre,' he said thoughtfully. 'The craft is so flimsy and unriverworthy, I feared we might be swept downstream into the western channel and be in danger of being swept on to the cataract. It is a small one, but dangerous enough to a craft this size and in this condition, but we must make the attempt. Sit very still in the prow and I'll push us clear. We will give the hippos a wide clearance, then I must struggle with the current to push back again towards the bank.'

It was a simple matter to push into midstream and for a while the current carried them swiftly, but Mern-ptah knew that in a short distance ahead a channel diverged to the west and it would be no simple task to steer the frail craft clear and move nearer to the Theban shore. He was tired and Yussef was inexperienced and unable to help. He allowed himself to rest for a while and gather strength for the battle which would come later.

He felt the pull of the counter current almost at once and exerted himself in a concentrated effort to steer clear of it. Yussef baled out bowl after bowl of thick yellow Nile water, while keeping as still as possible in obedience to the prince's instruction. For some moments, his efforts to guide the craft seemed in vain, then suddenly he was clear of the rapid current and able to make a course for the shore. Mern-ptah found himself drenched in a cold sweat of panic and offered up a prayer of gratitude to Ptah, the giver of life, to whose Temple they were journeying.

The rest was routine matter. Soon they encountered heavy Nile traffic and the first houses and temples hove into sight. Fortunately, there was space at the Temple's landing stage and he made fast and summoned a young server. 'Quickly, I need bearers, lad. This man is gravely injured. Call Ptah Hoten.'

The server's eyes flickered over his unkempt form. 'The high priest will soon be at his evening meditation,' he said coolly. 'I will summon assistance. If the priest on duty thinks he is required it will be for him to send for him.'

Mern-ptah caught him by the arm and stared fiercely into his eyes.

'Do you dare trifle with me? I am Prince Mern-ptah and need help for my slave. Do my bidding instantly. Time is short.'

The server's eyes flashed in amazement. For one split second he stared back, then recognising the authority of the man who held him, bowed hurriedly and sped across the garden to summon assistance.

Ptah Hoten came gravely to the landing stage. His eyes passed from the wounded man and back to the troubled gaze of the young prince.

'There was an accident at the new temple site,' Mern-ptah said briefly. 'Khefren could do nothing for the man. He has written what happened here.' He held out a papyrus scroll, which the high priest took with a slight bow, and read. He nodded quietly and signalled to the bearers who carried a bier.

'Convey him carefully to the healing ward. Try to move him as little as possible.'

Yussef made a movement to accompany his friend. Ptah Hoten glanced questioningly at Mern-ptah, who nodded.

'You may go with him,' he said gently, then paced quietly at the side of the prince as they followed at a slower rate.

'Has he haemorrhaged on the journey?' His question was calm and steady as ever and Mern-ptah took comfort from his presence. This man had always the spiritual authority to give him confidence and understanding when he most needed them.

'He has coughed blood once or twice. We gave him nothing to eat as Khefren instructed, not even water, though he begged for it.'

Quickly he outlined the happenings, which had led to the accident, confessing in a bald, youthful fashion, his own part in the affair and his feeling that he had handled events badly. The priest smiled gently.

'I see no cause to reproach yourself. You have done your part in bringing him quickly down river. I do not think Pharaoh will censure you when he knows the facts. You must be very tired. I think it better if you bathe and change, then spend the night within the Temple. I would not counsel you to present yourself to your father in your present state.'

'I will accept your hospitality, but I will wait and see how the slave fares.'

'As you will. I must operate to check the bleeding.'

Reuben, looking corpse-like now, had been laid on a limestone slab. Young healer apprentices had already cut away his clothing and cleaned him, ready for the surgeon's examination.

Ptah Hoten's examination was brief. The injured slave opened his eyes under the pressure of his sure fingers and the priest spoke soothingly, then rinsed and dried his hands and turned back to the prince.

'No bones are crushed, that is good. I think a small organ is injured and I intend to cut and investigate. If no vital organ is damaged, I should be able to prevent further bleeding.'

'Will he feel pain?'

'He is hardly conscious now. We will do our best for him. I will summon a priest to guard his Ka during the operation. It must be done — and at once.'

Yussef, ignoring etiquette, pressed forward and spoke to the priest.

'Will he die? Is it dangerous — what you do?'

'He is seriously hurt. You must pray the gods to give him their aid.' Ptah Hoten's expression was grave but kindly.

'Is there nothing *I* can do?'

'You are his friend?' Ptah Hoten glanced briefly at Mern-ptah, who nodded. 'Yes, you may stay. Are you sick at the sight of blood?'

'No lord — truly.'

'Then you may help me. Go and scrub your hands then stand near to the table. You may hold the basin while I work.'

Mern-ptah touched his shoulder, mutely giving permission and Yussef's eyes brightened at the thought of useful activity to still the ache of growing anxiety and he hurried off to obey the priest.

Mern-ptah moved from one foot to another, while he watched the silent group round the limestone slab. Unwilling to show his nervousness about watching the surgeons at work, he had forced himself to remain. He felt an odd nausea and pounding of his heart. In an effort to appear interested but unafraid, he drew somewhat closer. The priests had strapped down the injured slave and a young server stood calmly holding a tray on which was a collection of bronze knives and instruments strange to him. The Ka priest sat quietly, his eyes fixed and unblinking. The prince knew he would remain like this throughout the ordeal, ready to give his aid should the slave lose consciousness or die. By his special skill he could render the slave free of pain by his fixed gaze and use of repeated phrases. Yussef stood silent, holding a bowl of water and cloths to wipe away the blood, when requested to do so. He seemed entirely unconcerned, his gaze fixed now on the skilful hands of the healer priest.

Ptah Hoten murmured one or two quiet instructions and the server handed him a carefully honed knife. Mern-ptah swallowed hastily, as the priest bent over the boy and a scream rang out, which lapsed into a gurgled moan. The Ka priest bent over him, speaking steadily and the moans died down. Mern-ptah swung away, then turned back determined to watch. The priest drew the knife down the taut flesh, blood spurted and Yussef bent to sponge the wound. Mern-ptah abruptly turned towards the door, sick and faint at the sight of the healer's hands and the stains marring his white robes. He staggered outside and retched miserably. He had turned his face to the wall and did not notice the light patter of sandals or see the newcomer halt in surprise.

'What is it? Can I help?'

He turned suddenly, to see Asenath's look of concern change to amazement as she recognized him. 'Mern-ptah, what is wrong? What are you doing here? I thought . . .'

He swallowed again deliberately and straightened up. 'You thought I had been banished to the new temple site. So I was.'

'Then why are you here? Are you hurt?'

'No.' His answer was short, almost harsh, then he recovered his manners and bowed slightly. 'Forgive me, my sister. I must have startled you. I was — not feeling my best.'

Her eyes travelled past him, through the open door, to the group round the slab and he explained briefly.

'There was an accident on the site. They are operating on an injured slave. I fear I was not up to the sight.'

Her grey eyes opened wide. 'I see — one of the slaves — you say?'

'I deemed him of sufficient value to try to save his life.'

'Your tone is sharp, my brother. Do you think I would not agree with you?'

He smiled. 'Forgive me again. I am not myself.'

'Does father know you are here?' she asked quietly.

'No. Do you propose to tell him?'

'Of course not.' Her eyes flashed indignantly. 'You seem determined to offend me. I merely thought he would not be pleased.'

'True — I will present myself in the morning and explain, then return as swiftly as possible.'

'Mern-ptah.' He turned at the note of pleading he detected in her tone, and she continued, 'I was ashamed of my foolish conduct. Please forgive me. I am sorry you had to leave court.'

His expression was ruefully boyish. 'Do not concern yourself, Asenath. We were both foolish. The whole incident is forgotten. You still have Taia?'

She nodded. 'She is a delightful little companion, very willing to please. She is bigger already, now she is no longer half starved and ill-treated. You did well to bring her to us.'

'Then all is well.' He continued to look intently at her, as if with a stranger's eye, noting her budding loveliness and she stirred and flushed faintly, and was relieved to see Sen-u-ret, high priestess and wife of Ptah Hoten, approaching along the corridor. The priestess eyed

109

Mern-ptah with concern.

'You must come and rest at once. What a state you are in.' She turned. 'I think it wiser if you say nothing to Pharaoh about your brother's presence here.'

'We have already discussed the matter,' Mern-ptah said quietly. 'I will greet you tomorrow in the palace, my sister.'

'I must go — I shall be missed,' Asenath paused in her intentions as Ptah Hoten withdrew from the room and Mern-ptah turned to enquire about his patient.

'I cannot be sure. It is as I thought. I have cut out the damaged organ. He has a chance, but the bleeding has been heavy and prolonged. It is this which is our greatest enemy in the healing art. If the gods will it, he will recover. You brought him quickly, and if he survives, it will be because of that. Leave him now to rest.'

Asenath's eyes caught and held the dark ones of the Semite slave. She noted his proud carriage and aquiline features, so utterly unlike any slave she had encountered. He was not withdrawing himself respectfully, as was usually expected. His frown showed his concentration on the healer's report and *that* only. Momentarily, he looked full at her, and she flushed under his scrutiny, though she could not have said why, then his eyes flickered over her elaborately goffered robe of pale blue

110

mist linen, her jewels and her wig, then moved restlessly away again, back towards the room where his friend had been treated. She felt undressed in his presence and was surprised at her own embarrassment. He considered her a bedizened and painted fool and she was more disturbed at the thought than angry, as she had every right to be. She turned away to find Mern-ptah regarding her with a slight frown. She smiled and nodded at him and Sen-u-ret, then withdrew. Without requesting permission, Yussef moved back into the room and squatted down at Reuben's side. No move was made to prevent him and he sat as motionless as the sick man himself.

Sen-u-ret drew her young kinsman away to her own quarters and summoned a slave to bathe and annoint him with fragrant oils. He was pleased at the boy's attentions and gratefully stretched himself on the bed in the guest room to rest. The room was cool after the heat of the river journey and his body was refreshed and comfortable at last. He dozed somewhat and awoke to find Ptah Hoten smiling down at him.

'I see you are better. Sen-u-ret tells me you were unwell.'

'I was wretchedly sick at the sight of blood,' Mern-ptah confessed. 'I am recovered.'

'Your slave refuses to move from my patient's side.'

'You are angry with him?' Mern-ptah sat up at once, his frown showing his anger.

'Not at all. I am concerned for his welfare. He is in need of medical attention and he must be exhausted. I would be pleased if you would order him to rest.'

'Of course. I'll come at once.'

As they moved down the corridor, the priest was silent. Mern-ptah was not surprised. It was not Ptah Hoten's way to seek to know other people's affairs unless they chose to tell him. The condition of the slave's back concerned him as a healer, he made no judgements about sentences and punishments, leaving those matters to others whose business it was.

The prince paused in the doorway. Yussef sat perfectly still, keeping his watch. He did not turn at their entry.

'Yussef stand up and face me at once. You have been ordered away from the slave. Obey the priest, or I will have you flogged again.'

The slave turned unwillingly and looked from his master to the priest. Ptah Hoten's smile softened the harshness of the prince's utterance.

'Reuben is in good hands. It is unlikely that he will wake for hours and a healer is always on watch. You can do nothing for

him. Please leave him and come with me.'
He turned to Mern-ptah. 'I may treat him,
lord?'

'Of course. Go with the high priest,
Yussef, then attend me when he is finished
with you. You are not to enter the sick ward
again until I give you leave. You will only
be in the way of the healers and hinder
them in their work.'

Yussef bowed submissively and obediently followed the high priest. He sat down
in a small cubicle when bidden to, and
allowed himself to be cleansed and his
wounds treated. The priest asked no questions but merely spoke of what he longed
to hear, his friend's condition.

'Everything that can be done, has been
done. If he has a strong constitution, we
have little to fear. You did well during the
operation. Was that the first one you have
watched?'

'Yes, I watched Khefren the healer priest
on the temple site, at his work, but he did
nothing like that. I was interested and he
allowed me to help him with simple tasks.
One day I hoped . . .' he broke off and the
priest prompted him gently.

'You hoped?'

'That they would allow me to work as his
assistant, once the heavy building project
was over.'

'Why not now?'

'I have incurred heavy punishment, priest.'

'I see.'

There was silence for a moment, then the boy said in a rush, 'You have seen men executed?'

'Sometimes, when it was my duty to attend.'

'How long does it take a man to die — who has been impaled?'

'That depends on the man and on various considerations. The subject distresses you?'

'Yes. I made an attempt on the prince's life.'

'Yes?'

'It was because of the accident — I — I don't know why I did it — I don't hate him. I don't even think it was his fault — but I didn't think of anything — I just hit out with my mallet.'

'I see.'

'Would you plead for me, priest. If the prince was inclined to mercy, they would kill me quickly.'

The high priest stood up. 'I will certainly speak for you but I do not think you have need to despair. Had the prince intended that you should die, I do not think he would have brought you here. In the meantime, have no fears for your friend. Go and serve the prince well.'

Yussef found Mern-ptah standing in the guest room, watching through the open door, two small children at play in the courtyard. His body was once more clad in fine linen and exuded the rich smell of precious oils. He turned as the slave entered, a half smile curving his lips.

'You are better now the wounds are dressed?'

For answer Yussef slipped to his knees and kissed the slender fingers on one hand. Mern-ptah's voice sounded amazed when he commented on the action.

'You are in a mellow mood, master slave. What have I done to deserve that?'

'Everything you could to save Reuben. He will live because of you and he is the best friend a man could have.'

With a flick of his fingers Mern-ptah ordered him to his feet and then himself sat down on a chair near the door. He linked his hands behind his head and looked intently at the slave.

'My father had a slave called Nefren. He began by hating his master but he learned to serve him well. He is now free, lord vizier of the kingdom and my father's most trusted counsellor and friend.'

Yussef lifted his chin and gazed back at him. 'Why do you tell me this, lord?'

'Because a friend who will do what you did for Reuben, should serve me well, too.'

Yussef flushed and for the first time lowered his eyes in confusion. 'Lord, if Pharaoh discovers that I sought to kill you, he will order me executed.'

Mern-ptah smiled, the warm boyish smile his intimates knew well and loved. 'Then we must see that no one informs him of the facts.'

Yussef's proud face was briefly illuminated by a smile and he once more stooped and kissed the cool fingers of his new master.

7

Yussef rose from his prostrate position to stand well back in the shadows, while his master saluted his Royal Father and explained his sudden return to the court. The slave stole a glance at the harsh proud features of the great ruler of The Two Lands, who sat unsmiling and motionless until the recital came to an end. So this was the Divine Son of Ra himself. It was evident that even his son felt in awe of him.

There was silence for a while then he spoke quietly but so clearly that the sound seemed to ring in the pleasant airy apartment.

'I see. It appears that you obeyed my orders well enough and insisted on speedier progress. The accident was unfortunate. I cannot disapprove of your course of action. This slave accompanied you, I understand.' His gaze flickered over Yussef's submissive figure.

'Yes, lord. I would be grateful if you would release him from service at the site and assign him to me as a personal attendant.'

'It is more than time you began to order

the arrangements for your own household. Write an order giving your instructions. I suggest that he should be schooled in the usual manner.'

'Lord that has already been done.'

'Indeed.' Pharaoh's eyebrows were lifted slightly, but as his son gave no more details, he passed on to other matters. 'Have you seen Asenath?'

'Yes, lord. All is now well between us. It was only a misunderstanding.'

'Good. Remain with us for a few days. Your mother will be glad of your company. The supply boat will shortly sail for the new temple. I think it sensible if you account to only Rehoremheb. He will soon be able to start work on the colossi and you can leave him in charge, but first show the overseers your ability to keep your word and keep the work moving.'

'I think it wise to see that there are ample food supplies. The slaves were short of food. They cannot work to capacity under those conditions.'

'True. Order what you wish loaded on to the barge. I leave the details to you.' He picked up a papyrus roll, signifying that the interview was at an end and Mern-ptah bowed himself out.

He threw himself on to the couch in his own apartment, stretched himself and relaxed. There was no doubt about it. He was relieved that the audience had not been so painful as he might have imagined. He smiled across at Yussef, who stood waiting for instructions, his face grave. His thoughts were of Reuben, lying helpless, still in the Temple of Ptah. The healer priest had assured him that the slave would recover, but the hip bones would never knit perfectly and it was unlikely that Reuben would ever be able to climb up the swinging cradles above the pediments of the buildings where the skilled stone-carvers worked on their designs. Yussef was concerned for his friend's future. The prince's voice cut across his musing.

'I hope you will not need the schooling my father suggested.'

Yussef turned, his eyes opening wide. The prince's meaning had eluded him. 'Pardon, lord, I did not understand.'

'It is simple. Slaves are flogged when they join the royal household. It is customary as a lesson in submission.'

Yussef flushed darkly and Mern-ptah gave a light laugh. 'My mother is a gentle soul and disapproves of my father's harsher methods. The female slaves are spared unless it becomes necessary but my father schools his own personal attendants. Of course,' he broke off and smiled again broadly, 'he has never failed to teach his sons filial loyalty either. You will not be the only one who needs to fear his sudden anger.'

Yussef laughed in relief and squatted down by the couch. Mern-ptah propped himself on his elbow and outlined his plans for the loading of the supply boats with grain from the palace granary.

'You seemed unimpressed by the beauty of my future bride,' Mern-ptah said at last, as they idly rested through the heat of the day.

Yussef's chin jerked up. So the lovely girl who had spoken with them at the Temple, was a princess.

'She is my half-sister. Her mother was a Syrian princess who died when she was born. I am afraid she does not approve of my father's choice of a husband for her. We have quarrelled recently.'

'Could my lord not take a different bride?'

'No, she is throne princess, the Daughter of Isis. Only through her can I acquire the double crown. I shall not need to trouble her. I shall have other wives and concubines.' He smiled thinly. 'She appeared to be deeply interested in you.'

Yussef's attention had been given to the healer priests of the Temple. He had only half noticed the elaborately dressed court lady. He was sorry for her, forced into a distasteful marriage, then destined to be relegated to the harem and neglected by her royal husband and master. On considera-tion, her future held no more freedom of choice than his own.

The days passed quickly. To Mern-ptah, who was busy with affairs, they seemed to fly. His mother and Hotep-Re were de-lighted to claim some of his attention, and he passed no more than one or two polite words with Asenath. She appeared to be calmer, but still somewhat reserved and remote.

The short voyage was enlightened by the pleasant company of the master builder, Rehoremheb. He explained his plans for the temple. Two immense statues of Pharaoh were to flank either side of the entrance and he hoped to begin almost at once. They briefly discussed future designs for a new apartment for the Royal Heir when his betrothal to Asenath was officially an-nounced. Mern-ptah would then be able to command a small palace, possibly in the grounds, which were large enough to ac-commodate a lesser building, apartments for his attendants, guards, charioteer, and the women's quarters, where his wives and concubines would live apart from the men's side of the building.

Animated discussions took place about the accommodation for his pets. He wanted a large airy lion house, good stable accom-modation for his chariot horses, of which he was fiercely proud and quarters for his greyhound and hunting cats.

Rabu received him with state and was relieved to learn of Reuben's good chances of a fair recovery. Sickness had broken out on the site. No supplies had reached them and some of the slaves were near starvation. Mern-ptah gave immediate instructions to issue food rations and himself conferred with Khefren, the healer priest, about what was best to be done for the sick. It was decided to isolate them in hastily constructed huts at some distance from the rest and the priest was delighted with the supply of drugs and herbs, which had arrived from the Temple of Ptah. The fever was virulent but of short duration, he informed them. Once he had drugs and food to give his patients, he would be easily able to control the outbreak.

As Mern-ptah moved round the site, he was touched by the desperation on the faces of the toiling slaves. Urged on by his threats of punishment, the work had continued, though at a slower rate, and it was evident that Rehoremheb would soon be able to begin on his sculptured and decorative friezes to the pediments. He was horrified when he saw Yussef cradling his sister in his arms. Her flesh burned and was dry to the touch. She craved water and was near starvation point. Low as food supplies were, they had been issued only to the slaves healthy and strong enough to work. Touched by her pitiful fear of him, Mern-ptah carried her out of the foetid hut into the shade of the two palm trees. He fed her gently with mingled wine and water and summoned the healer priest. The girl was pathetically grateful for his ministrations.

By the third day most of the slaves were on the way to recovery. The worst of the heat was now abating as the river steadily rose, and heartened by the better food and diminishing discomforts, work again pressed steadily on. Mern-ptah assured himself that things would progress as his father hoped and prepared to return to Thebes. He took Ruth with them and determined to cause no more dissention or misunderstanding between himself and Asenath, conveyed her immediately on arrival, to his mother's apartment and requested that she would provide work for the girl. Serana at once complied and he withdrew, satisfied that Ruth's well-being would be assured.

On visiting the stables to bestow his customary affectionate pats and titbits on his chariot horses, he was surprised to find strange beasts in some of the stalls. Sidi, the chief charioteer, informed him that they belonged to the suite of the Hittite ambassador, who was visiting the court.

Mern-ptah frowned, 'Mardok here?'

'Yes, lord. He arrived two days ago. Pharaoh gives a feast tonight in his honour.'

'How long does he intend to stay?'

Sidi shrugged expressively and Mern-ptah thanked him for his care of his favourites, and left.

He dressed with care for the evening's entertainment and was gratified to note that Asenath was interested in his appearance. He grinned wickedly as she hurriedly averted her eyes when she caught his glance. As usual she was looking her loveliest in a gown of green mist linen and waving languidly an ivory handled fan of matching ostrich feathers. He thought her beauty enhanced by the slight childish pout, rather than diminished.

Mardok was seated close to Pharaoh and Mern-ptah was surprised to see that now he was no longer flushed and bloated by heavy drinking, he was a floridly handsome man. Dressed eleborately in purple silk embroidered with gold, he proved an impressive figure. The whole body was fleshy, he would run to fat in early middle age, but now he was a man to charm the ladies. His long black curls and beard were oiled to sleek perfection. The nose was beak-like, the mouth somewhat negroid in the thickness of the lips, but finely chiselled. Even in repose it was held in a hard line, and Mern-ptah could imagine what cruelties the man had imposed on the helpless Taia. Asenath seemed impressed. She had for once dropped her contemptuous bored pose, and was listening with rapt attention to what he was saying. Despite the respectfully lowered head and soft, suave manner Mern-ptah saw the Hittite's large bold eyes rake over her lovely form, revealed to perfection by the transparency of her fashionable gown. Naked desire flamed in those eyes and the watching prince felt vaguely sick and annoyed by her obvious appreciation of his manly attractions.

Yussef was feeling at peace with the world, as he made his way, late that evening, through the palace gardens in the direction of Mern-ptah's apartments. He had visited Reuben at the Temple of Ptah and had been the bearer of good news. The prince had demanded to know what was worrying him, and on learning that the injured slave would no longer be able to carry out his work of stone-cutting, had immediately made arrangements for him to work in the palace gardens, at least until he was more recovered and decisions about the hip could be made by Ptah Hoten. Reuben had been decidedly relieved, especially too on hearing of Ruth's new position as it would enable him to catch sight of her occasionally. Yussef knew his master would be late at the feast and lingered in the garden.

He rested near the ornamental pool to watch the light glimmer on the dark forms of the fish, then straightening up abruptly, listened to a whispered voice near-by in the bushes. The girl was pleading huskily with her companion. Yussef shrugged, but then stiffened, the girl did seem to need assistance. Her companion's voice was thick with wine and his heavy breathing reached the slave's ears though the pair were some distance away. Yussef's dilemma was clear. What right had a slave to interfere? The man was undoubtedly some official of importance, yet the girl's need was obvious. Her voice broke off into a sob. He moved in their direction and then stood still after parting branches of mimosa, to take in the situation.

The richly dressed man was obviously some foreign dignitary, for his long heavy purple robes and dark bearded face were not Egyptian. He had one brown arm round the girl's waist and was tilting up her chin with his other hand. She was clawing at his arm in an effort to release herself, and Yussef saw that her dress was torn and her elaborate wig awry. She spoke angrily now, commandingly, but the foreigner appeared to be too far gone in wine to heed her words.

'Fool, let go of me. At once.' She turned grey flashing eyes in the slave's direction. He was amazed that they showed no fear, only cold fury.

'Pull the drunken fool away from me,' she commanded him coldly. 'I do not wish to call the guard and make a scene.'

Yussef nodded in understanding and placed a respectful hand on the man's shoulder.

'The lady wishes you to return to the palace, lord,' he said quietly. 'May I help you?'

The man said something in his own tongue, laughed, and good humouredly tried to throw off the restraining hand, but Yussef tightened his grip and he turned, more angry now, and ordered him off.

The girl had released herself when he turned to the slave and she called out in cold anger as her would-be ravisher struck Yussef sharply across the face, the sound ringing in the quiet garden.

'Lord Mardok, you shame yourself,' she said. 'The boy is doing his work. You are drunk. Please leave us.'

The man turned back to her and threw out a hand to once more detain her, but appeared to think better of the idea. He smiled, but Yussef saw a strange glitter appear in his bold large eyes. He bowed, but even this respectful gesture was tinged with insolence.

'Your pardon, Princess. I have imbibed too well of your Royal Father's hospitality. I forget myself in my admiration of your divine beauty. Forgive me, I will withdraw.'

She bowed regally, a small frosty inclination of her proud head, then the man swept round once more to Yussef and his lips curved in an open sneer. The slave bowed low, but he stood his ground. He waited until the rustle of silken garments could no longer be heard and turned respectfully to the girl. He recognised her now, as she came further into the patch of moonlight, the Princess Asenath, throne princess of Egypt and Prince Mern-ptah's chosen bride.

'Thank you. You acted promptly. I was foolish to come into the garden unchaperoned.' She seemed unembarrassed and he admired the calm manner in which she pinned up the shoulder of her torn gown and spoke candidly.

'If you wish it, I will escort you back into the throne room, Princess,' he said quietly.

'Certainly. You are my brother's slave? Will you tell him of this incident?'

'Lady, I cannot think it essential that the prince should know of it.'

She drew a sharp little breath of relief and he saw more clearly what a child she still was, despite her regal airs.

'You will not tell him, promise.'

'I promise, lady.'

'It was very foolish of me. If the affair reached my father's ears, he would be angry.'

'I understand.'

'Do you?' She lowered her head and he was sure that her face was flaming with sudden shame. 'I was so stupid. He made a fuss of me and I let him, then when he brought me out here, I thought I could handle him easily. I had no idea he was so drunk.'

She fell silent and he waited quietly until she was ready to continue or made a move to rise. His eyes took in her youthful loveliness for the first time. When he had previously noted her at the Temple of Ptah, he had been too concerned about Reuben's safety to observe things or people around him. He looked for some resemblance to the prince but found none. Her eyes were large and grey, not fierce and proud like those of his master. Her figure would blossom to ripe perfection in the next year, already the firm high breasts strained proudly against the thin stuff of her robe. Her mouth was full; she would be generous with the gift of herself to the man she loved. Yussef had never looked upon a woman with the eyes of love, but he was stirred. He stood motionless however, until she stood up, her reverie over.

'Yussef, it *is* Yussef,' she said softly and reaching up touched with her linen kerchief a trickle of blood which oozed from the side of his mouth, where the Hittite ambassador had caught him with the sharp point of one of his rings. 'You are hurt. I am sorry I did not notice.'

'Nor I, lady — it is nothing.'

She glanced down at her own small hand, at her rings, anxious to choose a gift for the slave who had saved her embarrassment. Having read her thoughts and equally anxious to avoid such a moment, he glanced back towards the lighted palace. 'Do you not think you should return, lady? You may be missed,' he said hurriedly and she touched his bare arm lightly.

'I will not forget. If ever I can help . . .'

'Lady, it was nothing.'

'He will not forget. Watch him.'

He followed her at a respectful distance till she was close to the throne room, then he drew back and watched until he saw her laugh and ply her fan, talk easily about some subject of light moment to a guest and pass from his sight.

8

Yussef saw only glimpses of the princess during the weeks which followed. She had her own rooms in the women's quarters and appeared by the side of the Royal Wife at official functions and banquets. Once or twice he caught her eyes on him, as quickly averted, occasionally carrying a merry twinkle but more often in frank appraisal. In the silent dark hours, when he lay on his sleeping mat in the prince's apartments, he resolutely thrust thoughts of her aside. Was she not daughter of the gods, destined to be both Queen and high priestess? He told himself firmly that the idea did not hurt, but knew the denial to be worthless. He would never know such beauty or fascination in another woman. His heart was given for ever, and it was quite hopeless. If he could believe that Mern-ptah could make her happy, he would have rejoiced, but doubt nagged at his brain, and he feared for her. Alone among all the court the Princess Asenath, would defy Pharaoh in a desperate effort to secure her own happiness, and he knew the attempt would fail

131

and cost her dear.

Reuben arrived at the palace, limping but certainly recovered. He was slow at first, but he enjoyed the work in the gardens, finding a fulfilment in the care of the beautiful plants and trees, akin to that he had discovered in his working in stone. His gratification was complete when he saw Ruth, secure in the Royal Wife's service. She seemed well and happy and he was content.

Yussef was not the only one to concern himself about Asenath. The Royal Wife scrutinised her face as she sat staring out over the garden. Serana bent herself to the task of threading decorative beads on the frame of her small harp. 'You seem relieved that the Hittite ambassador has left court. I thought you admired him.'

'His tales were interesting, but he was a boaster, one to be neither admired nor trusted.'

'Mern-ptah openly expressed his dislike.'

'Indeed? Taia was terrified of the man. It seems he could be ruthless with helpless unfortunates and those who crossed him — but then — so is our father and Mern-ptah.'

'I do not believe that your father would deliberately inflict pain on others for his own pleasure.'

'Do you not? I heard yesterday that he

ordered one of the guards fifty lashes — the man almost died. My elder brother saw that the sentence was carried out to the letter.'

'The man fell asleep at his post. It was necessary as an example.'

'Could it not have been less severe, my mother?'

'I do not know, child. I have learnt not to think that I know better than your father. It is for him to secure not only our safety, but that of all those in The Two Lands. Mern-ptah must learn how to rule justly and ruthlessly, when the need arises.'

Asenath was silent and Serana touched her hand gently. 'You are feeling rebellious. Is it the nearness of your coming betrothal?'

'It is so decided then?'

'It wants only the official announcements. Your father will be obeyed. You will rule Egypt by Mern-ptah's side. Can you not accept the idea?'

Asenath shrugged. 'I must it seems, since there is no help for it.' Her eyes flashed dangerously. 'Though he may not find me a co-operative wife. I shall give him the double crown, no more.'

She left Serana's room hurriedly and moved out into the garden. The conversation had irritated her and she sought refuge in energetic exercise in the pool. She knew she could not relax in her apartment until she had tired herself completely.

She threw off her robe in a small secluded arbour, built for the purpose, and dived in. The water was cold and almost swept away her breath. She kicked out luxuriating in its welcome coldness. Normally she was an effortless, relaxed swimmer but today she drove herself to bursts of speed until, tired out, she made for the marble rim, too tired to swim further. There was no one to spy, so she pulled herself out and moved into the arbour for her discarded clothing, sat down for a moment until the moisture on her body dried in the sun's heat, then dressed and reached for her sandals.

Some shard of pottery or alabaster must have been left by a careless slave, for she gave a sudden cry of pain and stared down at her left foot, which was bleeding heavily from a long cut. There were no ladies or slaves in the vicinity and she put down a hand to staunch the bleeding. Blood welled through her fingers and she turned away for a moment, sickened by the sight.

It was there that Yussef found her. He spoke to her in an authoritative voice.

'Put your head down, lady. Right down. The faintness will soon pass. Let me see.'

She obeyed him, ashamed at her own weakness but too sick and faint at that moment to object. He lifted her foot and examined the injury carefully.

'It is not bad, but the bleeding must be

staunched.' He ripped off a portion of his linen kilt and made an improvised bandage. She sat up relieved to see that the blood no longer appeared to be pouring from the wound.

'I am sorry, that was childish. I think it was the shock. I am better now.'

'I will summon your ladies, Princess, and they will assist you to your apartment. You should not walk on this. It may need stitches and will be very sore.'

Asenath had recovered herself and was childishly inclined to tease the slave.

'But can you not assist me, Yussef? Surely you need no help to support so light a weight.'

Yussef hesitated. He was in a quandary. Well he knew, he should not approach the harem, but should insist on the presence of the princess's ladies, but it seemed churlish, even insubordinate to refuse his services.

'I would be honoured, Princess. Please put your right arm round my waist, so — that is it, now can you hop? It is only a step.'

'Very comfortably.' She dimpled at him and threw all her weight on to his sturdy frame. He was conscious of her small hand on his naked body and the clean fragrance of her hair and skin. He did not dare look at her in the simple robe and with her dark hair with its hint of bronze, hanging free and unrestrained, damp from the pool. Tendrils of it swept his shoulder and he ignored it, unwilling to note its beauty, free from the elaborate and heavy wig, in which she usually appeared.

It was a short step to the women's quarters and Yussef longed to call for attendance but she drew away from him and standing poised on one foot, placed a finger on his lips.

'No — not those chattering magpies, please they will fuss so. It isn't serious. If you will help me on to my couch, I can rest. I think the bleeding has stopped and it does not pain me.'

Embarrassed, Yussef supported her slight weight into her room and drew her to the ivory bed, heaped with silken covers and cushions, hesitated for a second, then lifted her easily into his arms and set her down.

He removed the soiled bandage and examined the wound again. It was not deep. If the edges were drawn skilfully together and bandaged with linen, on which a healing salve had been heaped, the wound would heal quickly and without a scar. He had seen Khefren treat wounds so, many times, nevertheless, in this case it might be wiser to summon a healer priest. She shook her head at his suggestion.

'I am sure you are a good enough physician. In the carved box there you will find some pots of salve and clean linen. Will you do it for me, please?' She was coaxing and he had no will to refuse. He busied himself about the room, found wine to cleanse the wound, water and the linen and salve. Trying to forget the sweetness of her breath as it fanned his neck, he gave all his attention to the task and bandaged the foot skilfully. She leaned forward to look, her lovely hair falling on to his head and mingling with his own dark curls. She professed herself satisfied and much more comfortable, and he made to rise, when she slipped awkwardly and fell forward, her arms by chance or deliberately, encircling his neck. Laughing, for a moment she clung to him, then her lips lightly brushed his forehead. A pulse pounded in his temple, as he fought with a longing to seize her and press his mouth hungrily on hers. She drew away a little and ran light fingers, soft as the feet of a butterfly, down one tanned cheek.

'Please, Princess,' he whispered, 'will you allow me to rise?'

She withdrew still laughing, then suddenly he saw her expression change. Horror darkened her eyes and for a moment she seemed frozen, unable to move. He stumbled awkwardly to his feet and turned to face the motionless man who had entered, unnoticed by either of them.

Pharaoh made no sound or movement. Yussef was aware of the rise and fall of his powerful chest, and the black scowl on the divine brow. It seemed no one could find words to explain the truth of what had happened. Behind Pharaoh stood a grave, quiet man Yussef knew to be the Grand Vizier, Nefren, next to Pharaoh the most powerful man in the kingdom.

It was Asenath who broke the spell. She slipped from the couch to fall at her father's feet.

'My father, lord, believe me — this was not what it seemed. I hurt my foot and the slave assisted me. He was bandaging it, and I leaned forward to look.'

Pharaoh was in no hurry to answer. He looked from Yussef to the kneeling girl, and his eyes held a steely glitter.

'I have eyes, Asenath.' He spoke without turning to the vizier behind him. 'Summon my guard and remove this man to the guard room.'

'My father, I beg of you. Yussef is guilty of no impropriety.'

'Yussef, you call the slave by his name?'

Asenath choked back a sob. 'You will not have him flogged — what he did was in all innocence.'

'Flogged!' Pharaoh lifted his eyebrows in surprise. 'You know well, Asenath, a slave who touches the person of a member of the royal household must die.'

'No — I beg of you . . .'

'Do not beg of me, Asenath. Your interest in the fate of this slave leads me to believe that what you told me was not true — that his presence here was not in all innocence.'

'I have no special interest in the man. You must believe me — he is personal body slave to Mern-ptah. He helped me, that is all. Must he die for that?'

'He dies, Asenath, because you kissed him. Do you deny what I saw with my own eyes?'

She turned from him, her lovely shoulders heaving with frantic sobs. Yussef knew it was useless to speak. He had not been addressed and he was too dazed and horror-stricken to offer one word in his own defence. By this time two guards had appeared in the doorway. Pharaoh clicked the fingers of one hand and the Grand Vizier motioned for them to lead him away. Pharaoh did not cast the slave even one glance, and he went submissively. The vizier withdrew discreetly and drew the heavy doors together, leaving Pharaoh alone with his weeping daughter.

He stood, waiting, his arms folded, then touched her briskly with one sandaled foot.

'Get up, Asenath. This is doing no good. Obey me, please.'

'I meant no harm. I was teasing the slave.

139

I knew he admired me and I kissed him. I have no feelings for him — I only tried to make him want me. I know it was wrong — please, you must understand.'

'I do understand, Asenath,' he said coldly, 'that I have not only a foolish daughter, but a wanton one, as well.'

'No — no, it was not like that.'

'Indeed.'

She stood up and faced him, throwing back her dishevelled hair. She searched his impassive face for a sign of weakening. He loved her well, and he usually gave way when she begged for favours. It was well to calm herself, and appeal to his devotion.

'My father, I have confessed that I was at fault. Please forgive the slave and punish me as I deserve.'

'I have punished you many times, Asenath, but it seems to have had little effect. You are no longer a child. Perhaps the fate of this slave will prove a lesson to you. A princess must not involve herself with anyone, let alone a foreign slave. He touched you, he desires you. He cannot be allowed to live. He must die a lingering death as an example to other slaves who harbour similar thoughts. That is my decision. I shall not alter my mind. Please refer to the matter no more. I must consider what is best to be done with you. Clearly you must be more carefully guarded. Your ladies and Mem-net have been negligent and must be reminded of their duties. I will see to it. Floggings will see that none of them forget their vigilance in the future. I shall send for you, later. For the meantime, regard yourself as a prisoner in your own apartment.

She knew it was useless, even dangerous, to appeal. She stooped and kissed his hand, then watched him withdraw. She stood for a moment, hands tightly clenched, her teeth biting so hard on the lower lip that the blood ran, then she moved to the bronze mirror, and putting back her hair, gazed critically at her tense, white face. There was no more time for tears. Only one thing could be done. Difficult and painful as it would be, it must be done if Yussef had any chance at all. She set herself to put her appearance to rights without delay, and summoned up her courage for the coming ordeal.

9

Mern-ptah smiled at his younger brother as he drew rein before the palace. The two had spent the morning wildfowling with great success. The evidence lay heaped on the floor of the chariot and his yellow hunting cat crouched beside them, fastidiously cleaning her sleek fur with a questing pink tongue. Hotep-Re stooped to caress her and she gave an appreciative purr of delight and lifted her pointed little face for him to scratch her under the chin. Grooms rushed to take the bridle rein and the two princes stepped down. Both were pleasurably fatigued and looked forward to relaxing under the skilled massaging of their slaves.

Mern-ptah looked up in surprise as Asenath came from the shade of an Acacia tree and touched his arm.

'My brother, I must see you at once. The matter is urgent.'

Hotep-Re glanced curiously at her white set face and the obvious disarray of hair and robe. She hardly seemed to notice him. Her whole attention was fixed on Mern-ptah. Hotep-Re murmured something about having business to attend to, and left them together.

'Please, my brother, can we talk?'

Mern-ptah drew her into his apartment and dismissed the slaves. He noted signs of recent tears on her lovely face which she had made vain attempts to camouflage. He made sure they were alone and then folding his arms, faced her and wasted no time in polite preambles.

'Well?'

'You must help me. Yussef is under sentence of death and it is due to my foolishness. He must not die. He is innocent.'

'Of what is he accused?'

She turned from him, biting her lip in evident embarrassment. 'Our father believes he was making love to me.'

There was no answer and she turned and looked appealingly at her brother's unsmiling face. 'You must believe me. It was not so.'

Still he remained silent and she pressed on. 'I . . . I had injured my foot . . . it was bleeding. I persuaded him to carry me to my apartment. He wished to summon assistance but I . . . I asked him not to.'

'Well.'

'After he had finished . . . I had leaned forward and . . . and,' she gulped nervously, 'I . . . I kissed him. *I* kissed *him*. He made no effort to touch me . . . but Father saw.

He has condemned him to die.'

'And why the concern?'

'Have *you* no concern for him? He is your slave. Do you care nothing that he will die for no reason?'

'Slaves can be replaced.'

'But not my conscience.' Her voice descended to a whisper. 'I did it deliberately. I played the wanton and not for the first time.'

'What!' For the first time he showed emotion, and swept her round by the shoulder to face him.

'I . . . I allowed Mardok to pay me compliments and led him on. . . . Please don't ask me why.' Her voice choked with sudden sobs. 'It was just a game. I wanted to see you angry and I wanted a man to say he loved me. It meant nothing.'

'To you perhaps. Are you a child, my sister, that you play on the feelings and desires of men and expect no repercussions?'

'I did not think. Yussef came then and interfered. Mardok struck him but left me alone. I owe the slave something. Please.' She sank to the floor and clung to his knees. 'You must help him. Father will not listen to me.'

He drew her to her feet and shook her sharply. 'Stop this crying. It will not help. Where *is* Yussef?'

'In the guard room, I think. Father ordered me to remain in my apartments so I could not question the guards.'

'And you disobeyed him? He will flog you, did you not know that?'

'It doesn't matter. Nothing matters now, only that Yussef must live. You will save him, Mern-ptah. I will do anything for you . . . anything. . . .'

He checked abruptly and a steely glint crept into his eyes. 'He will live. Return to your apartments and do *not* leave them. I will visit you when I have freed the slave.'

Yussef lay still and tried to forget the wrenching pull on his arms and his all-consuming thirst. They had fastened him by cords to bronze rings attached to a flat limestone block in the guard room. The cords bit savagely into his wrists and ankles but he was not really conscious of the discomfort. His head ached with the thoughts and doubts about the safety of the princess. Surely her father would not harm her. He had certainly been furious and would keep her close for a while, but she was blood of his blood — he would not physically hurt her.

The captain of the guard came over and tested the security of his chains. Yussef asked for water. The man shook his head regretfully.

'I can give you nothing till I get instructions from Pharaoh.'

'What will they do to me?'

The captain made to move away. 'I should try not to think about it,' he said gruffly, pity apparent in his rough manner.

Yussef's bowels turned to water and his body went icy cold. He must die, he knew that. For the second time in a few months, he forced himself to accept the fact, but if it could be quick and clean and he could be sure of the princess's happiness, he would have no regrets — but he would have liked Prince Mern-ptah to know that he had no intention of betraying him, yet it was unlikely that he would have any opportunity of explaining himself.

The door was flung open and by twisting himself painfully, he could see his visitor. Prince Mern-ptah stood in the doorway and surveyed him silently. Now that the opportunity was given, Yussef could find no words, but only appealed silently for him to understand. The prince strode forward until he was leaning down over the helpless slave. Briefly, Yussef saw the bronze knife gleam in the light from the open doorway, and prayed that the prince would strike true. The weapon slashed through the cords securing his ankles, then his left wrist. He was too dazed even to force his cramped legs to move until his master's voice spoke urgently, as he severed the last rope.

'Listen to me. I shall not repeat myself. My hunting chariot is outside the guard room. You will walk to it and climb in, then lie flat on the floor.'

'My lord I . . .'

'Spare me arguments. Obey me.'

Pain swept Yussef's cramped limbs as the feeling flooded back. He felt sick with the suddenness of the event, but he needed no further prompting, but got to his feet and followed his master. The captain made no effort to detain them and he limped to the chariot as commanded and crouched down. The prince strode in, took the reins from the waiting groom, and drove off. Miserably the slave half lay, half crouched, in the jolting vehicle. It seemed an eternity before the vehicle stopped and the prince spoke to him again.

'All right. You can stand up now and climb down.'

Yussef stumbled out into the sunlit street. They were in a quarter of Thebes unknown to him. The prince hammered on a house door with the ivory handle of his chariot-whip and a woman opened it. Yussef was ordered inside. The woman regarded him curiously but passed no comment. She was well past her first youth, but a handsome creature, heavily painted with great bold

147

dark eyes, which raked over his body, but showed neither dislike or approval. At a glance from the prince, she withdrew and left them alone in a small apartment in the rear.

'You will be safe here. Nofret follows a certain profession which carries the need for discretion,' he smiled as Yussef's eyes widened. 'She is utterly devoted to my interests. Indeed she initiated me into the joys of manhood.' The smile broadened at Yussef's unconcealed expression of horror. 'How naïve you Semites are. I was well recommended to Nofret. I could hardly betray inexperience in my own harem. Nofret knows that to betray me would ruin her position. Through me she enjoys a high standard of living and a flourishing good-class clientele. My father does not know of my visits to this house and so will not connect it with me. I command you to stay inside and never to venture into the street. I shall pay Nofret to feed you well. I will see what is best to be done. When it is safe, you must leave Thebes.'

'My lord,' Yussef appealed to him quietly, 'will you not ask me if the accusation was true?'

'If you wish me to. Was it?'

Yussef shook his head. 'I would never presume to touch her. It was a childish game on her part. She saw no harm.'

'She must learn.' Mern-ptah's voice was grim.

'One thing you must know before you risk yourself for me — I love her.'

Mern-ptah's chin jerked abruptly and his eyes searched Yussef's face intently. 'So . . . it is well,' he said and placed one jewelled hand on the other's shoulder. 'All is clear between us. She is mine. It cannot be otherwise. You understand?'

'I understand.'

'Then I will go. I will return when I have made arrangements.'

When Mern-ptah entered the palace, he was stopped by one of the harem eunuchs. 'My lord prince, your mother is anxious to speak with you.'

He nodded briefly and strode off to the Royal Wife's private apartment. He saw that she was deeply agitated and himself dismissed her attendants and taking her two hands within his own strong brown ones, he drew her to him and kissed her gently on the forehead.

'My lady mother, you look disturbed. What is it?'

'Mern-ptah what have you done? I cannot remember seeing your father in such a rage for years. He will tell me nothing. Asenath is confined to her room and he has forbidden me to go to her. Now he demands your

149

presence the moment you return. How have you angered him, my son?'

'Little mother it is nothing. Do not concern yourself. This is a private matter between my father and I. As for Asenath, she is a foolish child and has annoyed him. He will soon forgive her.'

'But what has she done? Does it concern the marriage . . . ?'

'No, my mother. Nothing will prevent my union with Asenath. Do not let this matter concern you.' She was trembling and he drew her to a chair. 'Beloved, you are cold, what is it?'

'Mern-ptah, I am afraid. When your father is angered he is dangerous.'

'Indeed he is.' Both turned to the brightly painted doors which gave access to the apartment from the main corridor. Pharaoh leaned against them, his arms folded, his beautiful sensitive mouth, held for once, in a hard cruel line. He was not wearing the double crown but the jewelled disk of Horus gleamed on his chest and even without the symbols of royalty, he made a commanding figure.

'Where is the slave?'

Mern-ptah made no answer and he moved slowly but gracefully into the room. 'Answer me at once. Where have you taken the slave?'

Mern-ptah was normally afraid of nothing, but he drew a little tight breath, then released his mother's hands, after patting them lightly, and turned to face his father.

'I regret, my father, I cannot reveal that fact until we have talked together. It was for this purpose I came back at once. The captain told you then, that it was on my authority, he let him go?'

'The captain was a foolish man. His stupidity will cost him dear. I will ask you again, for the third and final time. Where is the slave?'

Mern-ptah shook his head. Slight as the action was, it infuriated Pharaoh, who was unused to disobedience from even the most loved members of his family. He struck his son sharply across his cheek. The prince stumbled and fell and Pharaoh leaned forward to follow the blow. Serana sprang forward and caught his arm, clawing at him with her puny strength.

'My lord, please. This is your own son. Think what you do.'

He put her aside easily and spoke without turning. 'He is my son, my trusted heir, but by Ammon Ra I swear I will have him publicly flogged before the whole court, if he continues to defy me.'

'No.' Serana went white to the lips and knelt beside her son. Well she knew her husband would carry out his threat, despite all her entreaties, unless she could get these two furious men, whom she so dearly loved, to come to an agreement. 'Listen Mern-ptah, my son, you must obey your father. He is your ruler and his command is law. The slave cannot mean so much to you that he must come between you who love each other.' She dabbed at his cheek, where Pharaoh's heavy seal ring had left a bright red gash, reaching from the mouth to the high cheek-bone. He stood up, taking from her the linen square, and staunched the blood, then spoke quietly.

'Yussef is my personal body slave. He is mine to dispose of or punish as I wish. I must remind you of that fact, my father. If I am convinced of his guilt, I will order suitable chastisement. Do you deny me this right?'

'Both the slave and yourself are my subjects. Mine is the word which will be obeyed. I have passed sentence. The slave must die.'

'Because Asenath played the wanton and not for the first time?'

Serana gave a little cry of remonstrance but he pressed on.

'On her own confession. She is a stupid child who regrets her inexperience. She is my betrothed and it is for me to school her in obedience. Would you allow another to so school my mother, lord, even your own father had he lived?'

The tense line about Pharaoh's mouth relaxed and he turned and drew Serana into his arms. 'So — my lion cub is a man grown.'

'Man enough to deal with Asenath. When she is mine, I will do so.'

'I can see that it must be soon, within the month. It becomes evident that she is ripe for the marriage bed. But the slave cannot be allowed to see her again.'

'That I realise.'

Pharaoh smiled, his eyes softening as he tilted up his lovely wife's anguished face. 'And how will you deal with him?'

Mern-ptah hesitated for a moment. 'I would give him his freedom, lord.'

Pharaoh stared in astonishment. 'What possible advantage could such a course give you?'

Mern-ptah's smile was regretful. 'I was not thinking of my advantage, my father, but of his.'

Ramoses gazed full at his son, then he nodded. 'So be it. It is the best of all reasons, my son. You shall have it by the hand of my scribe within the hour. I hope you will not regret the act.'

Mern-ptah knew it was well to take his departure now. His father had only eyes for the woman who was his heart's joy. It was well to leave her to soothe the infuriated ruler, a task in which she had become proficient over the years. He blew her a light kiss and withdrew.

10

As Mern-ptah made to re-enter his apartment, a man withdrew from the shadows and threw himself at his feet. The prince's hand instinctively moved to his dagger-sheath but the man's voice arrested him in the act and reassured him.

'My lord, I crave but a word with you. I mean you no harm, believe me.'

The prince stooped to see more clearly the face of the supplicant, then relaxed and waved him to his feet. 'Reuben, you startled me, man. Get up.'

The slave climbed awkwardly to his feet. Obviously, the injured hip still troubled him. 'Lord, I beg you to tell me news of Yussef.'

'Yussef is safe.'

'I heard he was condemned to die. Lord, I know Yussef. He could not have done that of which he was accused.'

'I, too, know Yussef. All is well. I shall go soon to convey him to a place of safety. Pharaoh has granted me his life, but he cannot return to the palace.'

Relief showed on the slave's anxious

countenance. 'Praise be to the God of our Fathers. He will be returned to the building site?'

'No, I think not, but that I will discuss with him. You may return to your work.' He turned to move off then abruptly swung round. 'You work in the gardens. You like the work?'

'Yes, lord.'

'How would you care to attend me now that Yussef can no longer do so?'

The brown honest face was irradiated, as the slave leaned eagerly forward. 'Lord, I would be honoured if you think I could manage. I know nothing of the attention given to nobles. I have always worked with my hands in tile mines or at the building site. They are very rough and . . .'

The prince shrugged. 'You will learn. I am a firm taskmaster but not unduly impatient. Go and cleanse yourself, put on a fresh loincloth and return to my apartment. I will inform the palace overseer of my decision. Hurry now. I go to Yussef and you will see him.'

Reuben stooped and touched the ground with his forehead, then rose and in spite of his disability, hurried away.

Yussef was crouched in a corner of the room and sprang up at once when the prince entered. He looked quickly from his master to his friend, who followed, doubts expressed on his features.

'Do not fear for Reuben. He is not involved in disobedience. He comes with me as your successor, for you must leave Thebes.'

'Lord, is Pharaoh angry with you? Your cheek is injured. What . . . ?'

'Spare me your anxiety, Yussef. It was only a slight disagreement. You are reprieved.'

'But, my lord . . .'

'I have a gift for you. This scroll is your manumission. You are free. You may go where you wish but Pharaoh forbids you to enter the palace or hold speech with the Princess Asenath.'

'She is not harmed?'

'Not yet.'

'My lord . . .'

'*I* shall deal with the princess. She will soon be my wife. I shall rule her with a firm hand, but you concern me more closely at the moment. Freedom will not necessarily assure your well-being. We must find you work. It occurs to me that you may wish to go to the Temple.'

'They would take me?'

'Possibly. I suggest we visit Ptah Hoten. They have servers who assist the priests. You would learn and perhaps later, could be apprenticed to one of the physicians.'

Yussef's expression was incredulous. 'My

lord, I have always desired to learn the healer's art.'

'It is settled then. We will go to the Temple of Ptah. At the same time, I will get attention for this cut, otherwise it will leave a scar.'

Ptah Hoten received Yussef without commenting on the circumstances. He was glad to take the boy he said, as he had already noted his aptitude for healing. He examined the wound on the prince's cheek carefully, applying healing salve and gave advice as to continued treatment. As Mern-ptah offered no explanation of how he had come by the injury, he asked no questions. On being assured that Yussef would settle in the Temple, the prince left, attended by his new body slave.

He was amused to find Reuben most anxious to please. He laughingly excused the slave's clumsy first attempts to assist him in the careful toilet needed for the evening meal, dismissed him and scanned his reflection thoughtfully in his bronze mirror. The wound stood out prominently, but otherwise his appearance was pleasing enough. He decided to seek out Asenath and give her the information she anxiously awaited.

He found her at her toilet table, an attentive Taia brushing her bronze dark hair, an array of pots and jars open before her. The slave girl's eyes lit up at sight of him and she prostrated herself and kissed his jewelled sandal thong. He smiled benignly and dismissed her, at the same time ordering away the other attendants, as he wished to have private speech with his half-sister.

Asenath waited tensely for him to speak. He stepped back and stood regarding her admiringly. The slave girl had not yet completed her work and Asenath's face was bare of the costly paints which gave her the fashionable but uniformed appearance of the other women at court. Bereft of her elaborate plaited wig, she looked strangely childish and defenceless before him.

He reached forward and tilted up her chin, smiling into her eyes. 'Fear nothing. The slave lives.'

A little indrawn breath showed him the extent of her relief. She was concerned about nothing else, then her eyes widened and she stared up at the wound, livid in the glow of the oil lamp on her tiring table. 'You are hurt?'

'It is nothing. A mark of affection from our father.'

'He hit you — because you interfered?'

'Do not disturb yourself, my sister, you shall pay the price for it.'

She drew back apprehensive now at the mocking glint in his slanted black eyes, and he continued, amused at her evident discomfiture. 'Let me explain. Our father decrees that you shall be my wife within the month. I cannot believe that you will be pleased at that.'

'It is sooner than I expected.' Her tone was low, a little wary.

'But perhaps I am mistaken.' His smile broadened. 'It seems that you desire the attentions of a lover. Your recent escapades point in that direction.'

She sought to avoid his gaze and attempted to complete her toilet. She picked up a pot of eye paint, but he firmly took it from her fingers and replaced it on the table. She began to feel alarmed. It was difficult to know how to handle him this evening. He seemed different, his manner almost menacing. He had always previously treated her with a mixture of proud indifference and brotherly good humour, but since their first quarrel over Taia, she had begun to note the change in their relationship.

'You are very lovely,' he said at last. 'I can see how easily both Mardok and Yussef were captivated, but remember, little sister, these charms will soon be for my eyes alone. I do not wish a repetition of these occurences. I should be angered.'

'You will have your harem, my brother.' Her words were low but deliberately firm. 'I shall not concern myself about your relations with your other wives. I would be grateful if you extended the same courtesy towards me.'

'I am sure you would but I shall do no such thing.'

'That is unfair.' She was stung to a stormy reply.

'It may be so. It is unfortunate, but you will be my wife and if you impugn my honour, even by an indiscreet glance or word, you will smart for it.'

'You would not dare touch me. Our father will not allow it.'

'Our father will grant me the rights of all Egyptian husbands, to chastise my own property.'

She attempted to rise, her fear of him forgotten in a burst of rising anger, but he held her firmly in the chair by the pressure of his hands on her shoulders.

'Temper, little one, do not shout at one who will soon be your master.'

'Do you think I am a low-born slave to be treated thus?'

'It is the way of women to devote their love and obedience to their husbands.'

She forced a little half-embarrassed laugh. 'Do not be so unfashionable and naïve, my brother. All Egypt will laugh at you if you intend to treat your consort as a common dancing girl.'

'You wrong me, Asenath. I do not underestimate my dancing girls. I fully realise that they cannot perform well if their shoulders and backs are bruised and cut by my chariot whip. It is not so with you. You will not require such cossetting, so heed my warning.'

One last burst of defiance she threw at him. 'Mern-ptah, you have been drinking too much honey wine. I am grateful that you have saved the life of the slave, who meant nothing to me. Yet his death would have lain heavily on my conscience and I am glad of his safety. Do not count heavily on your ownership. I will give you the double crown with my hand in marriage, since it is the command of our father, but do not attempt to dominate me or you will rue it. I am Daughter of Isis, Princess of The Two Lands, and I will submit my will to no one, call no one my master, let alone a husband I cannot love.'

Her eyes were flashing with fury and he laughed as he swept her up into his arms and held her against his oiled body. She fought like a wildcat, raking her nails along his chest and tearing up at his cheek with her other hand. He gave a muttered oath as she caught the still painful wound, stood her down on the ground and caught both of her hands in one of his own.

'My hunting cat is wildest before she mates,' he commented mockingly, 'but she submits tamely at the end of the game. So will you and quickly. What will you wager on the outcome of the battle between us?' He was forcing back her head and shoulders till she thought her back would break and she gave out a cry of sudden pain. His lips were close to her own and she wrenched her head away, in a frantic effort to avoid them, then suddenly he drew away with a cool little laugh and put her from him.

'Forgive me, little sister, you call out the demon in me. I must wait.'

She stumbled back into the chair, her face flaming, too frightened and angry to cry.

He paused in the doorway, but as she had turned away from him, she was unaware of the strange, twisted expression which crossed his usually impassive features.

'Goodbye, Asenath. I will send your ladies to attend you. It is our father's wish that you should never be alone for one moment. It is an opinion with which I heartily concur.'

She made no answer as the door closed and she sat crying quietly, her tears splashing on to the powdered malachite prepared carefully for her use. When her old nurse entered the room, she reached out blindly in the old childish gesture for the solace of her comforting arms and gave way to harsh racking sobs.

11

Asenath was formally betrothed to Mern-ptah ten days later. Mern-ptah was declared officially the Royal Heir and for the first time donned the coronet of the office and mounted briefly to sit beside his father on the throne of The Two Lands. Pharaoh gave into his hands the crook of office, while he himself retained the sacred flail. At the same time, Pharaoh gave to Hotep-Re, the rulership of a Nome in the South and the promise of responsibilities and honours in the near future. He was well content and smilingly did homage before his elder brother.

Asenath's beauty seemed enhanced by the lingering sorrow about the eyes. She made her promises in a low and firm voice. Serana had feared hysteria, but the girl was calm enough, too calm for the Royal Wife's peace of mind. She summoned her to her apartment after the ceremony and strove to gain her confidence.

'You are very quiet. Are you still unhappy?'

'I think not. I must learn to accept my

destiny. My father sent for me after the affair with Yussef. You knew about that?' Serana nodded and she continued, 'I dreaded to face his fury, but he was more sorrowful than angry. He spoke of my duties and responsibilities and of my mother, how she had faced her lot with courage, obedient to her father's wishes. I began to see how foolish, even wicked I have been, to behave in so wanton a fashion.'

'Child you are no wanton.' Serana took her hand and squeezed it gently. 'Every girl of your age wants to be admired and loved. She teases her male acquaintances to give her proof of her beauty and her worth as a woman. It is natural enough.'

'But I must not behave as an ordinary woman. It is for me to sit by my husband's side and wear the insignia of royalty, but his other women will lie in his arms and bear his children.'

'Asenath, this will not be your fate. Mernptah will treat you well.'

'But he will not *love* me. He has already discussed the advisability of having children by me, with Ptah Hoten. The priest thinks children by his other wives will be stronger, perhaps because of our nearness in blood. Pharaoh's child by his cousin Nefertari was delicate and did not survive the plague. You know this.' She was silent for a spell, then she said quietly, 'I could bear anything if I could have babies.'

'This is what makes you unhappy?'

'The life of the harem is empty enough, but you had your babies to comfort you.'

'I had the great love of my husband.'

Asenath nodded and turned away, tears brimming her eyes. 'You had love for yours, while I only hold fear.'

Serana's lips curved into a smile of ineffable sweetness. 'No one feared your father more than I. It was not my will that I should remain in Egypt, but the birth of Mern-ptah gave me all happiness.'

'Your baby — yes. My mother died giving birth to me yet it was her fulfillment.'

'Your mother died knowing she had given everything to her lover. She wanted nothing else. His love was all she craved in return.'

'Yet she shared that love with you. I am too jealous to do that.'

'No, Asenath, she did not.'

The girl lifted her head and stared at her stepmother. 'I don't understand.'

'She did not. Her lover gave her all his heart.'

'But Pharaoh . . .'

'I did not say Pharaoh.'

'What are you saying . . . that my mother had a lover . . . ?'

'Would you blame her, Asenath?'

'But my father . . . he would have put her to death . . .'

'Yet he knew and did not. You will be my son's wife and Queen of Egypt, yet you have no royal blood of Egypt in your veins. Pharaoh is not your father, though he loves you as dearly as if you were indeed so. I will tell Mern-ptah the truth. You will have your babies, I promise. Will that make you happy?'

Asenath sprang up and seized her stepmother's hands. 'You tell me truly, he is *not* my brother?'

'You are not related in any way. I swear it. You need not fear to love one another. If your children die, it will not be because of nearness in blood. It will be the will of the gods and for no other reason.'

'Then Mern-ptah has no need to marry me. He will gain nothing by so doing.'

'In *fact* no, but in the eyes of the people, it will be so. Your father wishes it. You are a royal princess for your mother was the daughter of a line of kings. Your breeding is as fine as his.'

'But he does not *have* to marry me.'

'He *will* do so. Why should he not?'

She knew her stepmother's words to be true, yet her world had become torn apart in a few moments of time. She was too bewildered to ask further questions or even to gauge her own feelings. She murmured an expression of regret. She felt unwell. If her mother would excuse her, she would retire to her apartments and rest. She needed to think.

Serana was disturbed as the girl stumbled out. Had she made the wrong decision? Would Pharaoh censure her, even punish her, for revealing that which had been kept secret so long? It was a dangerous revelation and only her longing to comfort the desolate child had driven her to divulge it. The lovely Ashtar had been her greatest friend and her knowledge of the royal concubine's great love, had been their dearest confidence. It had drawn them together. She had sworn to love and protect this wilful, lovely daughter and that love had forced her to risk making what might be the greatest blunder of her life. Somehow, Mern-ptah must be made to understand, but she bit her lip as she dreaded the reaction which might ensue. She had not thought carefully enough before revealing the facts. Even her sons had grown away from her of late. She could not determine with any confidence what course of action Mern-ptah might take. If he repudiated the girl, what then? The thought sobered her, but even that would be better than this terrible loneliness to which Asenath was destined. Whatever the outcome, she could not regret her action. Surely, even Pharaoh would recognise this and in time, forgive her.

Asenath's thoughts were chaotic, as she fled from her stepmother's presence. She sought the peace of a quiet arbour in the garden and rested her aching head against the fluted column of its support. What would the prince say? He must know. He could not make her his consort, she was unworthy. She placed one hand against her eyes, as she thought of his mocking laughter and the proud contempt which would blaze in his eyes. Daughter of Isis, indeed. She was nothing, the byblow of an unfaithful concubine, who had charitably been cared for by a magnanimous husband. She had nothing to offer him. He could not even be sure of her fidelity. He would think her recent conduct explicable, when he learned of her parentage. If he did not marry her, what was she to do? She had no skill. She could not even keep herself. No honourable man would desire her in marriage if Pharaoh cast her from his household, yet she would not, indeed *could* not, stoop to plead.

She could not remain in the garden. At any moment, one of the gardeners might find her in a state of distress. She must return to her apartment, where she could think out what was best to be done. Memnet glanced at her curiously as she entered, but Asenath was in no mood for the old woman's idle chatter, so she cut her off sharply before she could ask searching questions. 'I am tired, Mem-net I wish to be alone.'

The old woman bowed and looked across the room, where a man's form was faintly outlined in the shade. He came forward, his pleasant voice polite but a little disappointed.

'I see my visit is inopportune, Princess. I will call later when you are rested. Perhaps you would be pleased to send for me at your convenience. I wish to discuss with you the plans for your private apartments in the new palace. The prince asked me to confer with you about your requirements.'

Always delighted to see the kindly master builder, Asenath was loth to appear churlish. Perhaps practical matters could for a moment, take her mind from the horror of her situation. She forced a smile and waved him to a chair.

'Rehoremheb you are welcome. It is too hot a journey to return again needlessly. Seat yourself. Give me a moment, and I will certainly give you my attention.'

He bowed gracefully. He was still a handsome man, tall and well proportioned, the muscles of the chest and belly made hard and strong with continued exercise, despite the touch of grey at his temples. He was thoughtful as she withdrew to dress herself in something more light and comfortable than the heavy court robe of metallic weave,

which she had worn for the betrothal ceremony. Something was disturbing the lovely
girl, who had always delighted his heart
with her merry laugh and roguish manner.
The ceremony was solemn certainly, and
she was of course fatigued, but her mouth
had been held in a thin tight line and dark
shadows ringed the great eyes.

She returned almost at once, outwardly
her usual charming self, and took from him
the papyrus scrolls and crossed to the open
front of the room, in order to study them
more closely.

'You will have a suite of rooms to accom-
modate your ladies as well as yourself and
the nursery will be placed — so. It is light
and airy but shaded during the heat of the
day. You approve?'

'Yes the plans are excellent. If they please
Prince Mern-ptah, I am more than satisfied.'

'This seems the moment to offer my con-
gratulations and sincere wishes for your
future happiness, dear lady.'

'Thank you.' Her voice trembled slightly,
as she turned away from him. Only one
whose ear was trained to note the slightest
tremor of distress in her voice, would have
noted the signs. He spoke respectfully but
anxiously.

'Something distresses you, Princess?'
'No, nothing.'

Her denial was quick and turning, she saw his tanned face clouded with love and concern for her and she reached out to the man who had ever consoled her childish sorrows, by his gentle kindness and understanding.

'Dear friend, I am so unhappy.'

Forgetting all etiquette, he folded her in his arms and she broke down into hard sobs, then little panted moans of distress. He waited, his face a mask of stone, then stroked her head, as if she were still indeed the child with whom he had often played.

'What is it, little one? You do not wish for this marriage, is that it?'

She stood up, and put a hand across her trembling lips. 'Tell me true, Rehoremheb. You say you knew my mother. Was she wanton in behaviour?'

Her face was turned from him and she did not see the agonised spasm which crossed his features.

'Child, who has spoken ill of your mother to you?'

'I am not the child of Pharaoh. My mother was unfaithful. Do not seek to keep the truth from me. It is so. I know it. How could she have done it? How dare she betray my father, her lord. It was unforgivable. I am glad she died. Had she not done so, her disgrace and shame would have been known the length and breadth of The Two Lands.'

He stemmed her impassioned outburst with a light but firm shake of her shoulder. 'Do not speak so of your mother, I cannot bear to hear it. You do not know what you are saying.'

'They taught me to love her,' she whispered. 'I honoured her.'

'And so you should do so. She was a great and lovely soul. Calm yourself, child, sit down and I will tell you about your mother. Perhaps when you know everything, you will be able to understand.'

'You said you knew her.'

'I knew her and honoured her. Will you let me tell you of her, everything I knew.'

Asenath nodded. She sank down on to the bed and he sat beside her, drawing her head on to his shoulder, in the old pleasant manner he had used when feeding her sweetmeats or displaying a pretty plaything for her delight.

'Your mother was given to Pharaoh as a gift by her father. She was never his true wife, but one of his possessions. When she arrived at the palace, she was apprehensive about the character of her lord, and dreaded to face life in the harem. However, she had been well prepared for her role by the devotees of Astarte. They had trained her well. She pleased Pharaoh and he favoured her. She found him proud and dominating and very lonely and she strove

174

to give him what he most desired, a child. It was not to be, but she proved a skilled bedmate and a cultured and understanding companion. She made herself content, but she could not give him all of her heart. You understand?'

Asenath gave an imperceptible little nod and he continued. 'She would have remained content, had she not met one day, by accident, the man who was later to become your father. They met in the market where she had gone to buy some material for a new gown. He saw her in the crowded street and life began for him from that moment. Nothing mattered for him any more but his longing to hold her in his arms and make her his own. You must understand that he did not know who she was and at first, she did not tell him.'

'That was dreadfully wrong of her.'

'Perhaps, but she loved him as completely as he worshipped her, and woman-like, she longed for a while, to keep him by her side. They met many times in secret and when he discovered her identity at last, he could not have stayed away from her if his salvation had depended on the outcome.'

'And I was conceived from their love?'

'When she knew of her danger, she could not regret. She told Pharaoh honestly, expecting nothing but dishonour and death at his hands. In his greatness, he forgave her and summoned her to his apartment, though he had himself then given his heart to the Lady Serana, who had borne him a son. Since your mother had been restored to favour, no one in Egypt doubted your parentage, and when she died, he mourned her in honour, burying her with his own dearly loved mother, and determined that you should lack for nothing and more than that, that Egypt should be your marriage gift.'

Tears welled in her eyes and she spoke huskily. 'I said what I should not. He loves me well, but what of my true father?'

'He loves you well too, Asenath. It has been the greatest joy of his heart to know your happiness.'

She turned slowly, staring up into eyes as grey as her own, then she put out a questing hand to his square cut bronze mane of hair. He held her close while she cried out her emotion, but her tears were warm and without bitterness now and gave surcease to her overcharged heart.

'I should have known,' she said softly. 'Your love has always been that of a father. Yours has been the greatest sorrow. She left you with nothing.'

'No, child, she left me everything; the memory of herself and our great love and now, the knowledge that my daughter can understand and forgive us.'

After Rehoremheb had left her, Asenath sat in the silent room staring out over the garden. Now that Pharaoh had ordered her attendants to keep constant vigilance over her, it was difficult to obtain privacy. She had begged Mem-net to leave her alone for a quiet hour and the nurse dismissed the ladies and herself stayed in the room next door, putting some finishing touches to clothes Asenath would require after her marriage. For once she had asked no questions, but seemed content to wait until the princess had need of her.

Strangely enough, Asenath felt comforted now that she knew the truth. The first shock of knowing of her mother's betrayal had made her angry, unrelenting in her condemnation. Now the affair, seen through the eyes of the master builder, who had loved her, seemed tragic and beautiful. Pharaoh's part in it was the most generous and kindly act of all. She had not thought him capable of such understanding. For the moment, she was not anxious about her own position, but sat drinking in the quietness, letting the peace seep into her very soul.

When Mem-net entered, she did not turn but said quietly, almost dreamily, 'It is all right now, Mem-net. You can come in and stay.'

'Lady, it is Prince Mern-ptah. He asks if

he can see you.'

'Of course.' Asenath wondered what her brother could want with her at this hour. Had his mother told him the truth, if so, what could she say to him?

Her nurse ushered him in and closed the door. He came forward into the lamplight and smiled across at her. He was carrying a small round basket made from papyrus reeds. He brought it over to her and set it down at her feet.

'I've brought you a present. You have had my official one of jewelry, but this is my real one.' Bending, he opened the basket and she stared down over his bent head, baffled by his attitude. He laughed up at her. 'Don't you wish to see?'

Like a child, she sank to her knees, then her eyes filled with sudden tears and she reached forward to take out the tiny hound puppy which blinked at her and gave a baby cry for attention. She fondled its silky grey coat and felt the rough pink tongue lick her arms.

'She's the finest of the litter. I was waiting until she was weaned.'

'She's wonderful, but won't you want the finest for the hunt?'

'No, the finest will be spoilt by your love. It is all I would ask for her.'

She sat back on her heels, the puppy clasped in her arms and he cleared his throat a little nervously. Now seemed the time to say what he had to say. With her hair swinging about her shoulders, and wearing the simple comfortable dress, she seemed once more the sister-companion he had known and played with, when they had both been very young. It seemed an age ago, since much had happened in between.

'I wanted to speak to you, my sister, but I could not while every eye was on us, earlier.'

'Yes?'

'I wished to apologise for my behaviour the other evening. It was unpardonable.'

'No — I was at fault.'

'We have both been at fault, of late, no more of that. I thought you might be frightened, unhappy. Asenath, you mustn't be. Neither of us had free choice in this marriage, but I swear I will be good to you. You have nothing to fear.'

She looked up at him, surprised by the sincerity and eagerness of his words. All traces of arrogance were wiped away. He looked anxious, intense, and yet the boyishness also appeared to have disappeared with the lock of youth, which he had shaved off that morning.

'When I came to you the other day I was angry. I threatened you. This morning I wished that none of those things had ever been said. You will be treated with every consideration and I hope that when I need your advice and counsel, you will be there to give it. I value your opinions. I shall not play the tyrant in my own home — unless you give me cause.'

'You had good reason to say what you did. You had the right to expect me to be discreet. I am sorry. I acted foolishly. I don't know what made me do those stupid things. Mern-ptah, will you tell me something?'

'Of course.'

'If I had not been throne princess, would you have wanted to marry me?'

He raised one eyebrow in boyish amusement and stood back to survey her critically.

'You are passably lovely, though you have a shrewish tongue. The figure is — pleasing.' Teasingly he paused before the final word, his mood now of brotherly provocation. 'I might have given a reasonable price for you, though a more docile wife would have cost me more.'

His smile faded as she did not rise and hit out at him in childish fun, as he had expected, but lowered her eyes to the puppy in her arms. He frowned in thought, as she remained silent, and noted the flush which had darkened her cheeks. Realising he had said the wrong thing, and uncertain how to proceed, he cursed his stupidity. He should have known that woman-like, she had wanted reassurance, not teasing. Bending he took the puppy from her, and replaced it in its basket, then drew her to her feet and cupped her chin in his hands.

'You are a most beautiful woman, Asenath. Every man who sees you at my side will envy me my possession of you, yet he will not know how your wisdom and understanding will lighten my life and be my greatest joy. Will that suffice?' His kiss on her forehead was devoid of all passion, an expression of his love and devotion. She blinked back her tears as she touched his hands in farewell, then he was gone.

The puppy gave a little whimper, and she turned back to it. He could not have known how his simple gift had touched her heart. He had the right to so much more, and she was cheating him. No royal blood of Egypt flowed in her veins and her place at his side and in his counsels, would be taken in dishonour. She could not tell him and she could not stay. She set down the hound puppy and summoned Mem-net.

'I shall retire now, Mem-net. Will you undress me, then retire yourself, you must be very tired.'

'Won't you want me to stay with you tonight?'

'No. Send me Taia, she is younger. You are so busy, with the plans for the marriage ahead. My women can also retire, I shan't need anything more tonight.'

It seemed an age before the women's quarters were entirely quiet. Asenath touched Taia on the shoulder and motioned her to silence.

'Taia, do you love me, truly?'

'With all my heart, lady. You have been so good to me.'

'Will you do anything I ask? Even if it is dangerous?'

The girl gave a single nod and Asenath continued, 'I am going on a journey. If my father discovers that you allowed me to do so without giving the alarm, he would punish you severely, even put you to death.' She avoided the alarm in the child's eyes. 'Therefore it is best if you go with me. Do not be afraid. I have a protector and I will take care of you.'

'You are leaving the prince, lady?'

'I must, for his sake. Will you come with me?'

'Yes, lady, if it is what you truly want.'

'Then come. We must pack a small bag of necessities only. I can buy more later. Find me my plainest gown, no jewelry. I do not wish to be recognised in the streets of Thebes.'

12

Rehoremheb was not a heavy sleeper and he sat up alert at once, when his slave shook him gently, anxious to deliver what was obviously a message of some importance.

'There is a young lady, sir, asking to see you. She has a slave with her. She will not give her name. I did not like to refuse her admittance. . . .'

Rehoremheb cut short his explanations and reached for clothing. 'You have done well, Hamid. Admit the lady to my workroom and take the slave into the kitchen for food.'

Hamid bowed and withdrew, while Rehoremheb hastily attired himself and hurriedly went to the study. Asenath put back her hood as he closed the door and held out both hands to him.

'I have come to you in my need. You will not fail me.'

'Child, what is it? Are you in trouble?'

'No — but I cannot stay in the palace.'

'Mern-ptah — he has hurt you . . . ?'

'No, no,' her lip trembled. 'No, if that had

been the case, it would have been easier to stay.'

'I do not understand.'

'Oh, Rehoremheb . . . I love him so.' She turned away, though he could hear her quietly crying. 'I cannot cheat him into marrying me, nor could I stay to see his contempt when he knows the truth.'

'Sit down, child. I think you must explain to me slowly, what is distressing you so. You say you have had no quarrel, that he does not know. . . .'

She shook back her tears and sat on a bench by his side. 'No — he came to me with a gift. A hound puppy. He was so considerate. I could not tell him. If he could choose, he would make someone he loved Royal Wife, the mother of his son perhaps, or Pharaoh might choose for him one of our cousins, one more fitted to be Great Royal Wife than I.'

'Asenath, you are Pharaoh's choice. If you leave now, after he has arranged this marriage, you will make him very angry. Do you not think you owe him something for the long years of caring for you?'

'He will understand how I feel. He loves me.'

Rehoremheb shook his head. 'I love you, Asenath, but I cannot understand your motives at this moment. You say you love Mern-ptah, yet you do not wish to become his wife.'

'It is *because* I love him, that I do not wish to become his official bride. He will honour me, but not love me. I could not bear to live in his house and see that. Will you take me away, please, Rehoremheb. I have no one to turn to but you. You will help me?'

He stood up and turned away from her. His thoughts raced with the dangers she would bring upon them all. Looking at her now, listening to her pleading, he could see and hear again the lovely woman who had held his whole heart. When Ashtar had loved she had thought nothing of the disasters to come. Their child was like her. If he could have persuaded her to give herself time, he might have headed off her intentions, but he knew he had no hope of that. Childishly and passionately, she would set off alone, or if that were not possible, even take her own life if there were no one by to prevent it. His heart turned cold with fear at thought of Pharaoh's fury. If they were caught? There would be no mercy for him who had deliberately defied him. Where could he take her? Yet they must leave Thebes and at once.

He swung round and squeezed her hand. 'Smile, little one. There is nothing to be afraid of. If go you must, why then we go.'

She expelled a little sigh of relief and he smiled. 'That is better. I have made you happy again. Stay and rest. It would be wiser if I put you to bed. I must collect enough valuables to keep us for a while.'

'I had not thought — I came without money — not even my jewelry. I deemed it not truly mine.' Her distress was evident. She had thought nothing of even how she was to live.

'Hush, child. I am not a poor man. Now I have the chance to keep my own daughter. Come to my chamber and rest. I must arrange for our journey down river.'

She seemed content to trust him utterly. He stayed by her for a moment until, spent with emotion and fatigue, her head slipped back on to the head-rest and he knew she would sleep. His private barge was at the landing stage. He summoned his steward and gave him instructions.

'I have heard of some difficulties at the Temple of Ptah in Per-Ramoses. I intend to take my barge down stream and investigate. There is a problem about one of the support pillars. Order the crew to load supplies for the short journey to the Delta. I would embark before dawn if possible. I should be back within a few days.'

The man accepted his orders without complaint. If the early hour of departure seemed strange, he passed no comment. Hamid had told him briefly of the cloaked woman who had come in the night. He could keep a close mouth when discretion was needed. His ability to keep his own counsel had granted him his master's favour in the past and would do yet again. He gave the necessary orders and averted his eyes when Rehoremheb drew the two discreetly garbed young women down to the landing stage and gave orders for the boatmen to cast off.

The chill air of morning woke Asenath fully and she sat on deck as they passed the misty outlines of the city buildings. It was too early yet to see much, but she could just distinguish the walls of the outer courtyard of the Great House and the fluttering pennants on the pylon of the Temple of Ptah. She steadfastly refused to think about her own future. It was enough for the moment to allow her dear friend and blood father to think out ways and means for them both. Pharaoh would be angry and bitter. Serana would be sorrowful as Hotep-Re would be also. Mern-ptah would be annoyed at first that she had caused him scandal, but time would take the sting from his pride and he would be secretly pleased that he might choose his own Royal Wife. No doubts about his right to the succession could disturb him. He was officially the Royal Heir and on occasions, co-equal with Pharaoh.

She glanced down at Taia who had slept

curled up in her cloak, at her feet. It had been uncharitable to bring the child into uncertainty and danger, but she needed one link with the palace. Mem-net could not have left her beloved Mern-ptah, and it seemed most fitting, that she should take with her, his first gift, and the one which had caused her first to consider him as a man with whom to be reckoned.

Over the meal Rehoremheb outlined his plans. 'It seems wise to take you first into Midian. I know a wealthy sheik there, who would offer us hospitality. I am a skilled architect. It should not be difficult to obtain employment, and for the present, I have enough to establish us in comfort.'

She leaned forward to take his hands and conveyed them to her lips.

'Dear, dear Rehoremheb, do not think that I accept lightly the sacrifices you are making for me. I know well what it will cost you to leave my father's court.'

'Child, for me it is a simple matter. I only pray to the gods you will not regret your own decision.'

There was no answer to that, and she forced a smile. 'You think we will be pursued.'

'I think it likely.'

'Pharaoh knows that you . . .'

'Yes — he knows.'

'Then you will be his first suspect.'

'Probably.'

'I did not think of your danger. . . .'

'Give your heart peace. We have a fair start. You will not be missed for some time yet. My steward will give good reason for my absence from my house. He will make no mention of my night visitor. There will be time. If we can reach the Midianite caravan and one leaves promptly, there will be little danger.'

'But the caravans only leave on certain days.'

'Then we must hire camels and drivers of our own and set out at once. Do not panic. Trust me. Go into the cabin and try to sleep.'

For all his reassuring words to Asenath, Rehoremheb was by no means at peace. Pharaoh would not lightly dismiss this act of defiance. It was more than likely that pursuit would be swifter than he might have anticipated. Would it be wiser to leave the barge at the next landing stage and change direction? To take a public boat upriver and stay for a while at some village until the chase died down, might be a wiser course of action. He could travel as a master craftsman accompanied by his two daughters. Pursuers would then follow his barge. Possibly Pharaoh's chariots would take the desert route to the Delta to cut off his escape. In that case it would be several days before their absence from the barge would be noted. The more he thought of it, the more sensible his later plan appeared. He summoned his boat captain and quietly told him what he wished him to do.

Asenath did not question his decision as he hustled the two women and Hamid off the barge at the next village. Leaving the slave to guard the two women, Rehoremheb went to make enquiries about public transport further up-river. Asenath had never been allowed freedom to wander unrecognised through the streets of Thebes though she had often gone quietly to the Temple of Ptah with her slave Boda, and it was a new experience to watch the village people about their business. Several small craft plied from shore to shore carrying onions, melons, figs and large bundles of papyrus. Asenath was relieved to note that the people seemed happy enough, despite their days of unending toil. When Rehoremheb returned, he seemed pleased and informed them that a public boat could convey them up-river later that afternoon. They found a small tavern where they were able to buy a simple but palatable meal and wait under the shade of a trellised vine in its small garden, until the noon heat abated.

The boat was large but crowded. Asenath shook her head, smiling at him, as Rehoremheb ruefully guided her to a seat on a box, avoiding baskets of strong-smelling onions and herbs and one which emitted loud squawking sounds. It was not what she was used to, certainly, but the journey held no less pleasure for her for that.

Later, Taia laid out for them on a linen kerchief, small hard loaves, cheeses and onions and a flask of cheap wine. Asenath was unusually hungry and found the frugal repast very satisfying. They were so intent, that at first, they did not notice the intense stare of a man who stood by the tiller, and watched them. He had noted the little group earlier, how they kept to themselves and seemed unlike the poorer peasants who formed the majority of the ship's passengers. It was the taller of the women who interested him. Surely he had seen her before and remarked on the beauty of those large grey eyes and dark hair with its strange hint of copper. She had been dressed more elaborately then, but he had remembered that hair with its simple but expensive golden circlet as being so effective, outstanding in the Egyptian Court, when so many of the other women had worn those large elaborate wigs. At the feast of course, it had been hidden by the wig, but sitting by her father earlier at the Hour of Audience he had been struck by her artless yet sophisticated taste. Mardok too had remarked on her charms. He would wonder, as did his steward, what she could be doing on this boat, accompanied only by so small a retinue. He had believed that the women of Pharaoh's house were very closely guarded. He stored the information for future reference and resolved to discover where the party intended to lodge. It would be worth his while interrupting his own journey on Mardok's business to discover her destination. He felt sure that his master would not censure him for such a course of action and smiled to himself.

13

Pharaoh looked fondly across at his wife as she sat in the early morning sunlight. Her brows were contracted in thought and he leaned forward and touched her arm lightly.

'What is it, have I caught you inopportunely by so early a visit, my wife?'

She turned at once, a sudden smile illumining her lovely face. 'My lord jests. He knows it is unexpected joy to me to receive him whenever he chooses.'

'Then why the frown?'

'Was I frowning? I did not know it. I was thinking.'

'Of Asenath?'

She laughed. 'You are a mind reader — yes, of Asenath.'

'The girl behaved well enough yesterday. She appears to have accepted the situation.'

'She can do nothing else for she has no choice.'

'Mern-ptah has sworn to be good to her.'

'I know it. I trust him, but it does not always help. It isn't enough. Asenath is

Ashtar's child. She has a passionate nature and I fear for her. Sooner or later she will rebel and what then?'

'Mern-ptah is my son and I am sure he will know how to deal with her.' He frowned imperiously as a whispered consultation outside the door warned him that officials threatened to intrude on his brief spell of privacy. The frown darkened as the door was thrust open and Mern-ptah burst abruptly into the room. Without waiting for leave to speak, he closed the door and advanced towards them.

'It is well I find you together for I must speak to you urgently. Asenath has left the palace. Mem-net came to me some minutes ago. I have been down to the river with Hotep-Re. She is not in her room. Mem-net is convinced she did not sleep there.'

'But that is impossible, Mern-ptah.' Serana rose to her feet agitatedly. 'How could the girl have left the palace? She may have risen early and gone to the Temple or be walking in the garden.'

'Mem-net has searched thoroughly. There is no sign of her. She has avoided causing a fuss and indeed waited to tell me first. Taia is also missing.'

'But why — what could have happened? She . . .'

'You quarrelled after the ceremony?' Pharaoh's question was demanding.

'No, my father.'

'You saw her — afterwards?'

'Yes indeed, I went to her apartments.'

'Why?'

'I wanted to talk to her privately. I swear I said nothing to upset her. I wanted to reassure her about the marriage. I took her a present, a hound bitch puppy.'

'Did she seem distressed, Mern-ptah?' Serana's voice was quiet, but insistent.

'No, my mother. I did not think so. She was tearful when I teased her. . . .'

'You teased her?' Serana's interruption was sharp.

'Yes, she asked me if I would have chosen her if she had not been Throne Princess and . . .'

'Then I am to blame. Dear lord, I should have told you earlier.' Serana drew away from them, tears springing to her eyes.

'You told her the truth?' Pharaoh spoke coldly without emotion.

'I had to. She was so distressed. She wanted children and Mern-ptah was against the conception of children so near in blood. She dreaded to live a lonely, barren existence so I told her. I promised that we should tell him. . . .'

Mern-ptah stared from one to the other. 'Tell me what? I do not understand.'

Pharaoh waved his hand for the two to be seated. 'It is simple, my son. I intended to

195

explain the truth before your wedding, but there seemed enough dissention at present to suffice. I wanted to tell you when I could be sure that you would understand. Asenath is not my child. She discovered this yesterday, and I suspect has left the palace in panic.'

'Not your child — you mean she is not my sister?'

'Just so.'

Serana had thought quickly. 'Where could she have gone?'

'Did you tell her the name of her father?'

She shook her head at her husband's question. 'No, she did not know, I am sure.'

'Her father was known to you?' Mernptah's expression was incredulous. 'And he still lives?'

Pharaoh took him gently by the arm and looked into the young eyes, as fierce as his own. 'One day, you may understand. At your age I too would not have done so. Remember, I never asked that Ashtar should love me, no more than you expect Asenath to love you. She loved another and I forgave her. Do you question my action?'

'No, but if he himself knows, how has he kept it so long from Asenath? He has seen her?'

'Rehoremheb has seen her frequently but I am sure he has never revealed his relationship, though many times he must have

196

burned to do so.'

Mern-ptah drew a swift breath. 'Rehorem-heb? He visited Asenath yesterday.'

'Are you sure?' Serana's face expressed sudden hope.

'He expressed his intention to do so. He brought me the plans for the new palace. I requested that he consult Asenath about her wishes. He said he would do so immediately.'

Pharaoh nodded briskly. 'Then if she were upset about your disclosures, my wife, it is possible that she confided in him and he told her the truth.'

Mern-ptah was eager. 'Then it is likely she went to him.'

'Likely enough. I will dispatch the guard to his house.'

'No, my father.' Mern-ptah held up a warning hand. 'There must be no talk in the palace. This must be kept to ourselves.'

'One question, my son.' Serana took one of his hands and looked at him directly. 'Now that you know, are you content with this betrothal?'

Pharaoh made a gesture of anger that his wishes should be questioned but she shook her head slowly and waited for her son's reply.

He put up his other hand to touch her bright hair. 'I love Asenath, my mother. Perhaps this explains a great deal but I will not talk of that now. She will be my wife and bear me sons, if the gods will it. We must get her back and at once before news of this leaks out. You agree, my father?'

'Perfectly. You are right. Mem-net must be sent for. We must say that Asenath is indisposed. In the meantime, call at Rehoremheb's house. If he has taken Asenath, then they will already have left, but there may be some clue to their destination. Return to me here as soon as possible.'

Mern-ptah stooped and raised his mother's hands to his lips. His lips were tensed but his eyes smiled. 'Fear nothing, little mother. I shall find her and bring her home. The gods help her when I do, but she shall not escape from me, I promise you.'

She did not seek to hold him but bit her lip as he withdrew and turned frightened eyes to her husband. This foolish action of hers had caused a complete disruption of his plans. Even her concern for Asenath could not dispel her alarm. Years ago he had severely punished her for disobedience of his command and those actions had been relatively minor compared with this interference. He drew her into his arms, and stroked her bright hair.

'Calm yourself, little one, you meant well enough. My anger is all for Asenath. Nothing can excuse her conduct. She is indeed

Ashtar's child. We must wait patiently now, until Mern-ptah returns.'

Rehoremheb's steward was more than a little surprised to receive Prince Mern-ptah enquiring for his master. The prince's expression was grim and he wasted no time in stating his business.

'I wish to see the master builder. Tell him the prince demands to see him immediately.'

'I regret, lord, my master is away from home.'

'When will he return?'

'He did not inform me, lord.'

'Come man, where is he?'

'My lord, I . . .'

Mern-ptah seized the unfortunate slave and put his face close to his. 'If you wish to please me, you will tell me where he is — if you do not please me . . .'

The implied threat caused the man to tremble. It had not occurred to him that his master's amorous intrigue could have angered the prince. He decided that it was unwise to disemble.

'My lord, he planned to travel down river to the Delta. There were problems at the Temple of Ptah and . . .'

'He was accompanied by a lady, a *young* lady?'

'Two ladies called late last night but . . .'

The prince released him abruptly and

turned to a member of the royal guard who had accompanied him.

'Keep that fellow in the palace guard room. I want no gossip about my visit here.'

The soldier nodded stolidly and hustled the man away. Mern-ptah made a brief but thorough search of the house. He was not expecting to be successful. Rehoremheb would undoubtedly have already conveyed Asenath from Thebes before the alarm was given. He would know it was his only chance. He strode through the rooms of the elegant house, regardless of the curious stares of the household slaves, then returned to his chariot and headed once more for the palace.

He waited impatiently for the Hour of Audience to end, and was thankful at last to see his father eagerly enter his apartment. On learning Mern-ptah's news, he considered for a few moments silently then nodded.

'It is as I supposed. I myself will visit the Delta. Men-ophar can accompany me with a small detachment. If we cross the desert, we shall be there before them.'

'We must leave at once.' Mern-ptah moved to prepare himself but his father's harsh voice arrested him in the doorway and he turned back.

'I said *I* would go — alone.' The word was final and Pharaoh raised a hand to still his son's urgent protests. 'I want no scenes. No hint of scandal must touch Asenath and I will deal with Rehoremheb in my own way. I will brook no argument, Mern-ptah. I command you to stay and deputise for me in my absence. Your mother will need you. Asenath will be gravely unhappy. If you attack her now, your lives together will be marred by ugly memories. Believe me, Mern-ptah, I know what I do. Trust me.'

'I do, my lord. You speak wisely, but I wish I could find a reason to dispute the matter with you. I shall eat out my heart until you return.'

Serana's distress was evident as she took leave of her husband, though outwardly she strove to give the impression of a routine parting, since he was to investigate building problems in the Delta. Once in her room, after his departure, she gave way to tears and Mern-ptah roughly attempted to comfort her.

'Pharaoh will return her to us, do not distress yourself.'

'He will do that but I fear for others. Rehoremheb will suffer for this and I feel I am to blame.'

'My mother, this is not so. Asenath is a foolish child. Who could think she would behave so?'

'I should have known it. At her age, I would have behaved just so. Men will never understand the workings of a woman's heart. She felt shocked, rejected, and she ran.'

'Her training as a princess should have taught her self discipline.'

'Mern-ptah, you are your father's son.' Her reply was tinged with exasperation and he turned to her in bewilderment and she waved away his demand that she should explain herself.

For three days Mern-ptah fumed impotently while he awaited news from the Delta.

It was Mem-net at last who conveyed an exhausted Taia to his room. She saw at once the urgency of the child's need.

'My lord, my lord forgive.' The girl fell at his feet sobbing. Her clothes were dirty and torn and her hair dishevelled. He noticed that she had difficulty in walking and Mem-net had half led, half carried her into his presence.

The girl's distress came second to his burning desire to know what had happened and he jerked her to her feet, not heeding her cry of pain.

'Tell me at once, where is your mistress? What are you doing here?'

'My lord she is with Mardok.'

His fingers bit into her shoulders and she caught back a second cry.

'Tell me, tell me at once.'

202

'His steward recognised her. It must have been on the barge. That night they attacked the house we had rented. They killed Hamid and the other slaves and they took the lady Asenath and the noble lord Rehoremheb with them. I jumped from the window and hid in the bushes till I could get to you.'

He shook her to still an outbreak of weeping. 'Where have they taken her? All this is incomprehensible. You must tell me briefly but slowly everything that happened since you left the palace.'

The child looked up at him, her eyes terrified. Never had she seen his face so grim. He had no thought for her pain or fear. She forced herself to be coherent.

'Lord Rehoremheb conveyed us down river at first. It was his intention to reach the Delta, then he left the barge as he feared Pharaoh's chariots would overtake him. We went up river again by public boat and stopped at a little village about five miles away. It was very quiet. We hired a house near the river. It was secluded and Lord Rehoremheb believed we would be safe there for some weeks until the chase died down. It was a pleasant house and my lady seemed almost calm, though she cried a lot when no one was watching. I noticed though she tried to hide the signs from me. We thought no one had seen us. We did not leave the house. Only Hamid went to do the shopping and he hired some servants then last night . . . they . . . they broke in. There was screaming and blood . . . and my lord tried to fight but they bore him down and chained him. I recognised Mardok's steward. He did not see me. The Lady Asenath ordered me to jump from the window, though she would not leave the master builder. I hurt my foot in the fall but I hid and saw them take them away by boat then I ran to the river and a fisherman brought me to Thebes.'

'They will take her to his villa. Was Mardok with the party?'

She shook her head. 'I did not see him or hear his voice commanding the men. My lord knows — I know it well.'

'Little Taia you have done right to come to me at once. Do not weep that you left your mistress. It was best that it should be so. How else would we know?'

'They killed everyone, so that no news could come to you,' she shuddered. 'I heard them while I . . . while I crouched in the garden. It was dreadful I . . .'

'Fear not, little Taia. All of them shall be avenged and fittingly. Do not cry any more. Mem-net will take you to the princess's apartments and we will send for a healer priest to deal with your injury. You are not to repeat a word of this to anyone. If anyone asks why you were absent from the palace, you can say that you went on an errand for your mistress. No one will ask, I think. The princess's ladies know well the need for discretion.'

She looked at him appealingly, and he touched her arm in a gesture of comfort, a fleeting smile touching his grim lips, then he sounded the bronze gong, to hand her into the royal nurse's charge and to summon the captain of the guard and his slave, Reuben.

To the captain he handed a sealed dispatch. 'Deliver this to Pharaoh in the Delta city by your fastest courier and await his orders. Ask my father's sailing captain to attend me here.'

If the man was puzzled by the prince's air of urgency, he made no comment but hurried at once to obey. Mern-ptah spoke briskly to Reuben. 'I want clothes for travel and suitable sandals, a supply of food for two days at the most, my hunting knives and war dagger. You will accompany me. We travel light.'

When he had changed for the journey, his mother was announced. Though Memnet had given her no details, she came at once, anxious to know if he had news. He told her briefly what had occurred, while he completed his preparations. She went white to the lips, and sank down on to a low chair, her eyes following his movements, hurried but orderly.

'I shall go after her. I shall take my own boat and our sailing captain as I need skilled handling of the equipment. I may need to concentrate on other matters. I have informed my father by dispatch of my intentions. If I do not return with Asenath in three days, he will know what to do.'

'But you will need help.'

'I shall take the best. Fear nothing. A detachment of cavalry would not be of assistance — yet. It would only endanger Asenath further, and she would be hopelessly compromised.'

'But what can you do — alone?'

'I know the house and if necessary, I am trained to kill.'

'My son, would Pharaoh send his Royal Heir into danger?'

'I do not know, my mother, only that, if it were you and not Asenath in that house, he would not hesitate for a second to go himself. I leave Hotep-Re with you.'

She could only obey him and pray for his safe return. As his captain had by now presented himself, she stood up to take her departure. He took her into his arms, a sudden impulsive, almost lover-like gesture. Recently he had not demonstrated his affection so openly and she clung to him, while she dared, then gently released herself and left him.

14

While his light sailing craft was made ready, Mern-ptah went to the Temple of Ptah. He found Yussef, in the sick ward, assisting the priest on duty. At a sign from the prince, the server put down the tray he was holding, spoke softly to the priest and followed his former master into the corridor.

'I have need of you. Asenath has been abducted. I go to fetch her home. Will you come?' The words seemed half wistful, half appealing.

'I may ask Ptah Hoten's permission to absent myself, lord?' Mern-ptah nodded briefly, then he walked calmly away.

In the servers' room, Mern-ptah watched while Yussef carefully stowed away a pot of salve, a linen roll and a sharp knife in a small satchel fastened below his waist. The former slave gave a brief explanation. 'We may need them if one of us is injured.'

'Did Ptah Hoten ask questions?'

'None whatever. When he knew you had need of me, he gave permission at once.'

'He did not ask after Asenath?'

'No.'

'It is only that we have given out that she is ill. He may have wondered why he was not summoned to attend her.'

Yussef said quietly, 'He knows more than any one of us chooses to tell him. I am ready, lord.'

While the young sailing master set the indicated course, Mern-ptah held a council of war. Each of the men in the party knew his need and the necessity for speed and silence. They listened without comment to his unemotional account of what had happened.

'We must get Asenath clear of the house before any attack from outside. I do not know the building well but I have visited it once. I shall leave you, Namu and Reuben here in charge of the boat. I want you to draw as near to the villa landing stage as possible without being seen. Yussef and I will proceed on foot. Then withdraw to this village on the plan I drew. There is a landing stage. We cannot bring the princess by water, as the ship would be an obvious target. We will come the short journey through the desert to join you in the village. It should not be difficult if she can walk. If not, we must carry her.'

He paused for a moment while they digested the instructions, then the young captain said quietly.

'How long do we wait for you, lord?'

'It should only be a matter of hours.' Mern-ptah shrugged eloquently. 'If we do not arrive, await Pharaoh's orders. He will know what to do and should be back from the Delta in two days, three at the most. Chariots are fast across the desert and the courier will not slacken pace until he reaches him.'

'But you will need inside help, lord.'

'If we are not clear of the house by day-break, it will be useless to try to aid us.'

The two in charge of the boat withdrew to the stern, leaving the prince and Yussef together. They were silent for a while, watching the curved prow cleave the water smoothly. Mern-ptah was thinking ahead, striving to make plans. He had sounded sure enough of himself, but in reality the whole exploit was fraught with risk. Asenath might already be dead. He refused to consider that possibility; or heavily guarded, which was likely although the Hittite Ambassador considered his surprise abduction to be unknown to the palace officials. Speed and surprise were the only likely elements to aid him. A formal demand from Pharaoh himself might be later expected, backed up by armed force, but the possibility of the infiltration of two men, might prove successful, by the simple fact of its utter rashness. He decided there was little he could do until he reached the house and made some assessment of the situation.

Yussef's thoughts raced beyond the possible success of their mission to other matters which concerned him more.

'You will hardly expect to find the princess confined in a guard room of sorts,' he observed.

'Mardok's room is near to the one to which I was assigned. It lies to the rear of the house, away from the river, facing the garden.'

Yussef was satisfied that his doubts had been squarely faced. The prince looked at him directly.

'I read your thoughts, my friend. You have already considered that we might be too late.'

'I do not fear for her life. Mardok would hardly . . .'

'Even that I have considered. He might do just that, if he wishes to deny to Pharaoh any knowledge of her whereabouts.'

Alarm sprang to Yussef's eyes. 'That did not occur to me.'

'You were over-concerned by doubts as to my reaction.'

'If she is dishonoured . . . ?' The words were whispered so softly that Mern-ptah guessed at their import rather than heard them.

'Asenath will be my wife and the future Queen of Egypt if she lives. Nothing else is of any importance.' He smiled at Yussef's little sigh of relief, then turned and conferred with Namu about speed and currents.

The desert night was about to descend in its suddenness, when the small boat was pulled into the bank, under the shelter of close-growing reeds. The dark shape of the house could be glimpsed on the next bend. The prince and Yussef slipped unobtrusively overside and swam then waded ashore on the western bank. Namu then pushed off into midstream, in obedience to his orders.

The house was aglow with oil lamps and the two crouching watchers saw the slaves and officials moving about their business across the courtyard. Food was apparently being prepared in the kitchens and the efficiency of the workers suggested that the master himself was in residence. Two foot soldiers stood on watch by the gate and it was probable that others guarded the ambassador's private apartments and were in attendance in the dining hall. A torch gleamed on their bronze helmets and leather body armour. Mern-ptah placed a hand on Yussef's arm. His companion nodded, indicating that he had seen them. The prince led him silently to the eastern side of the garden, away from the stables and guard rooms on the far side. Large grain bins loomed above them but no servants were in evidence to draw supplies and this wing of the estate seemed uninhabited. There was no sound of music or laughter from the house, so Mern-ptah imagined that no guests had been invited. The two had found it simple enough to help each other over the low hedge and into the grounds themselves. Mern-ptah had only an imperfect impression of the house's grand plan, but he was never entirely un-observant and he knew clearly enough in which direction the luxurious apartments and official rooms lay. The room he himself had occupied, which was undoubtedly kept as a guest room for noble and important visitors, appeared empty. No chink of light appeared from the windows which led directly into the garden, but farther along, where he thought the ambassador himself had his sleeping chamber, he could hear sounds of movement and saw a glow of light, though the door was closely shuttered, an unusual occurrence on a night so warm. Was Asenath within? If so, her presence would indicate the need for the barring of the door-way. Only an unwilling guest would wish to remain so cloistered on such a night. He crept close to his companion so that he might bend and whisper directly in his ear.

'I believe that is Mardok's room. It is shuttered, so Asenath may be confined there.'

'It will be guarded on both sides. Can you see movement in the bushes outside?'

'No, but I imagine you are right. The guard will be quiet so as not to disturb his master.'

'You think the inner door will be watched?'

'Undoubtedly. Mardok will take no risks of intruders invading his privacy.'

'And the master builder?'

'Difficult to say. I think it unlikely he is with Asenath. They could already have dispatched him. He would be of little use to them.'

The prince eased his cramped position and once more surveyed the quiet garden.

'I think the best means of entry might be through the guest room. It appears dark. I imagine it to be unused this evening. Its inner door gives on to the same corridor as Mardok's room.'

'But that corridor will be guarded.'

'Then we must tackle the guards. They will hardly be expecting us. Ready?'

Yussef nodded decisively as the prince crawled over to an opening between young cypress trees and peered out.

A guard was standing outside the window, leaning negligently on the hilt of his

213

spear. Mern-ptah considered what was best to be done. The man did not appear formidable, but if he dispatched him simply and neatly, as he was confident that he could do, the man's absence would be noted. Likely he reported to someone in authority or was relieved at intervals. The last thing Mern-ptah wished to do was to draw attention to his presence in the house and a body, however neatly bestowed, would be discovered within hours, even minutes, and broadcast to the owner that an intruder was trespassing on his property. It would be wiser to divert his attention or wait for an opportune moment. It seemed that the favour of the gods was with him, for round the corner of the building a young slave girl came into view. He could only catch a glimpse of her in the darkness, but he judged her to be comely, as the guard made what appeared to be a jocular remark, and he heard her giggle in answer. While the man's back was turned, and his interest elsewhere, he ran lightly to the guest room, pushed open the bracket which held the two shutters across with his drawn knife, looking anxiously about him, as a slight click betrayed his action. The guard either did not hear or considered the sound not unusual, for he made no effort to investigate. The prince crouched quietly in the doorway, then moved further into the room.

A moment later he heard Yussef join him, and moved softly to guide him round the heavier objects of furniture, whose positions he vaguely remembered from his previous visit. He heard talking and laughter from the corridor so knew that he must cope with hostility on the other side.

He judged it was not yet late enough for the ambassador to retire. It was possible that the noise was emanating from the dining hall not far away and though problems would be encountered, he knew his only chance to find Asenath alone, would be now, before the party still feasting broke up.

'There will be a guard on Mardok's door,' he said quietly. 'I must tackle him now. Later will be more difficult. Wait for me here. Join me if you hear no undue noise, or come if I do not return.' He eased his dagger from its sheath and cautiously opened the door.

The corridor was lit by torches set in brackets at intervals and was empty apart from one young man who stood with his back to the door of the ambassador's chamber. He turned at once, as he heard the door behind the prince, swing to, his eyes widening in astonishment. Strangely enough, he made no attempt to cry out or even withdraw into the room. Mern-ptah remembered him as the slave who had waited attendance on Mardok during the feast and who had later assisted the drunken official to his bed-chamber. He waited calmly until the prince's advance halted within inches of his body, the deadly blade close to his heart.

'Is Mardok within?' The prince's voice was no less deadly, despite its softness.

'No, lord.'

'If you cry out, I shall kill you.'

'That I realise.'

'The lady, she is in there — alone?'

'Yes, lord.' The slave smiled momentarily. 'Do not fear. I will not betray you. To meet death would be welcome to me, so if I wished to, I would.'

'You have the key?'

For answer, the slave drew out the bronze implement and himself turned it in the lock. 'If you can save the girl, I pray my gods you may do so, but I do not think you can leave the house. It is crawling with armed men.'

'Let me see her, then I will consider future action.' Mern-ptah paused just once before entering. 'You would change masters, my friend?'

A dull flush touched the thin cheeks. 'What would you have me do?'

'Admit the man who waits in the guest room, then stay on guard until I call you. Give warning of any other who approaches.'

'It is well, lord.'

Asenath had been secured by ropes to the high silk-draped bed. She gave a harsh sob as the door opened and in a flash, he had come to her side and placed a hand over her mouth. Her agonised grey eyes stared up into his own, until he released his hand, feeling before he did so, the salt wetness of her tears. He sliced through the cords and drew her to a sitting position.

'I knew you would come, yet I feared it. Mern-ptah . . . please, you must leave me . . .'

Behind him he knew Yussef waited and wasted no time in attempting to comfort her. 'Has he hurt you?'

'No. Only tonight he returned, but he will be here soon.'

'I know.' She caught her breath at the sudden ferocity in his tone. Blood was pulsing through her cramped limbs and she caught back a cry of pain.

'Yussef, see if the slave outside knows anything of the master builder. He will be our man, if we trust him.'

Yussef nodded and obeyed. Mern-ptah turned to the crouching girl. 'I know you are cramped, but you must walk.' He stooped and picked up a silken cover, tearing it in two with his teeth. 'Put this round you and pin it. You are half naked.' They had painted her and annointed her lovely body and dressed her in trousers and close fitting jacket of the shimmering, transparent material he knew was silk and came from far across the world.

She obeyed him but said quietly, her tone strangely lacking emotion. 'You must leave me I say. I cannot come back with you.'

'Asenath, I have no time to argue or even to plead with you. Obey me. Our safety depends on it.'

'The gods know how you have given me all I longed for — you came. I deserved that you should leave me to my fate, yet I prayed that you would come. I am content, but dear love, you must go. You cannot save me.'

'Then we will die together, all of us. We are sworn to this. Can you doubt that we would do otherwise?'

'No, I do not, but I am beyond help. I will explain. Within a few hours I shall be beyond pain or dishonour. Look, my brother.' She pushed forward her left leg and he saw a small purple mark, hardly discernible on the ankle. Yussef pushed by him and examined it, carefully.

'Dear God who has no name — a scorpion,' he said huskily. 'Lady, how long?'

'Some hours ago. I stamped on it deliberately. Please, Yussef, you know what this means. Take him away.'

Mern-ptah drew him away to the door. 'What can we do? Can she walk?'

'Lord, I do not know. The sting may be deadly. It depends on the species. Some cause only discomfort — others, death. Some slaves at the building site recovered but most do not.'

'Did the priest treat them?'

'Yes, but he said himself it might do no good. A fatal sting causes convulsions, then death within hours.'

'What did he do?'

'It is difficult to remember. He cut the wound, I think, and cauterised it — but . . .'

'You can do this?'

'Here?'

'Now, at this moment. It would be madness to wait.'

'We shall be discovered . . .'

'You are afraid?'

'Lord, you shame me, but she will scream in agony.'

'Not if I gag her.'

'You would do that?'

'I will do what I must.'

Yussef nodded. 'You are right, but we must carry her afterwards. It is likely she will lose consciousness.'

'Perhaps the better for our purpose.' Mern-ptah's voice was grim.

Yussef waited for no more but looked around the room for implements he could convert for his purpose. He fetched the oil lamp on the carved chest over to the bed

219

and drew from his small satchel a slim-bladed bronze knife.

Asenath watched his preparations with mounting horror, then turned agonised eyes to her betrothed husband. 'What is he going to do?'

'Listen to me, Asenath. Look at me. Give me your hands. Yussef is going to hurt you — very much, do you understand?'

'No — it is useless, please Mern-ptah, you impair your own chances of escape. My father and I are doomed.'

'No, we all leave together or none of us. I have sworn by Ammon. You must be brave, for if you scream, we shall be discovered.'

'Mardok will kill you.'

'Perhaps, I doubt it. If the gods will it, I shall not complain.'

Yussef looked up and nodded significantly. Mern-ptah moved round to the head of the bed and gathered Asenath's slender form into his arms. She had gone very pale, but resolutely turned from the sight of Yussef's equipment.

'I will not cry out, if you hold me tight,' she said quietly.

'It will matter little if she does, lord. A cry will not be noted in this house.' The slave's quiet voice came to them from the doorway.

'Then stay on the outside and warn us of anyone approaching.' Mern-ptah tightened his grip on Asenath's shoulders. He was sitting on the bed with her upper body held hard against him. 'Turn your face inward and bite into my shoulder. That's right. Yussef, get on with it.'

He felt Asenath writhe in his arms as the knife cut down, then stifle a scream against the hard muscles of his upper chest. When he laid her back on the bed, sweat was pouring down her face and her features were contorted. He could not have believed she could have endured such pain without an outcry. Yussef skilfully bound up the wound and fetching wine, held it firmly to the girl's lips. She shook her head but he insisted, and she swallowed painfully. Mern-ptah stooped to wipe away a trickle of blood from her lower lip, where her teeth had bitten down savagely, in the final spasm of her agony.

At the same moment, the slave jerked open the outer door.

'My lord, there are sounds that the meal is about to end. You must hurry. Mardok will be here within moments.'

15

Mern-ptah withdrew Asenath's clinging fingers. 'Tell me, man, who enters his bedchamber?'

'I do. I assist him to undress, unless he is so drunk that the guards help carry him.'

'I think that unlikely — tonight. Very well, my friend. Go back to your post. Assure him that all is well and admit him as usual.'

The slave bowed and obeyed.

'Gather up your belongings, Yussef, and get behind the bed. In the shadows over there. I see you have a knife. Pass me that leopard skin on the bed.' He caught the heavy rug lightly and deftly arranged it on his arm. 'Now Asenath, listen well. All you have to do is to lie back. He will not notice from the doorway, that you are not bound. He will not be surprised to find you terrified. Keep your eyes on Mardok when the doors open and nothing else. You understand?'

She nodded. Her body was shaking with icy chill, but she knew she must obey him. She pulled another of the exotic silken covers over her bandaged leg and lay down to wait.

They could hear the sound of noise and laughter from the dining hall. Asenath closed her eyes and prayed to Isis to aid her. She knew that Mern-ptah waited silently by the door. He was so calm she could not even hear him breathe. The stillness was oppressive, then Mardok's voice could be heard along the corridor. He was talking in his own tongue with another man. She thought she recognized the voice of his guard captain. Panic welled up again. Would the armed captain enter? What choice would Mern-ptah have in such a contingency? She steeled herself to remain calm.

Mardok challenged the slave at the door, who answered respectfully. Apparently he was satisfied for she heard him laugh loudly and he dismizsed his captain. The slave swung open the door and the Hittite paused before entering.

The light from the oil lamp on the tiring table illuminated his form clearly. He had dressed with care in brilliant scarlet. His bearded lips parted in a smile as his insolent black eyes flickered over her tense form. He was in no hurry to advance further.

'It distresses me, dear lady, that you cannot rise to greet me, as I am sure you are anxious to do.' His voice was urbane, studiously courteous.

She trembled and swallowed nervously and he spoke again. 'This is the first time I have known you without words, Princess. Come now, they have not gagged you. Some little word, a token of your esteem.'

She forced herself to look at him, as he moved gracefully forward. Her fear for the moment, wiped out the burning agony in her leg. She curled her lip and said disdainfully, 'Do you expect me to cringe before you, Hittite scum. I do not weep for what you can do. My father has his own methods of avenging wrongs.'

Mardok came to the bottom of the bed and smiled down at her. 'Doubtless he would, if he knew that he *had* been wronged, but who will be left to inform him? It is so sad that the whole of your household met with unfortunate accidents. You yourself? Ah, dear lady, I have not decided yet what will be best for you — later, but it will be a great deal later, before I tire of you.'

He was not drunk, but she felt his wine-scented breath fan her cheek as he bent forward. Mindful of Mern-ptah's instructions, she kept her eyes on his face, as it loomed above her, then it was gone and he was being inexorably forced back struggling helplessly in the folds of the heavy leopard skin. Mardok had been completely relaxed, intent upon his prey, so his hand had not moved in the direction of the fold of material on his hip where his dagger lay hidden. The attack had been expertly handled and complete. He was enmeshed in the stifling, heavy covering. His captor held his arms in a merciless grip which tightened slowly and surely.

'My lord Mardok underestimates the divine power of Pharaoh. He knows the second he has been wronged and moves to punish.'

Mardok's blood froze at the sound of that young yet singularly harsh voice, which carried a note of deadly pleasantry. He could make no reply. He was doomed and he knew it. His men were within feet of his presence, yet he was helpless to utter a sound. Had he not known the girl herself would bring about his destruction? In all his life he had never needed to sue for love. Only this girl denied him and for his overwhelming desire for her, he would die.

The prince was speaking now, yet more softly. 'It distresses me, Lord Mardok, that our acquaintance should end so abruptly. Had I the power to offer you the hospitality of my father's guard house, we would linger awhile in friendship, but alas, you will understand my need for haste.'

He leaned backwards, bringing his powerful muscles into full use. Mardok felt himself forced back and back. . . . The agony was unbearable. He knew himself to be silently screaming into the rug which had rendered him helpless. The sudden snap brought him release and Mern-ptah stood up and allowed his dead weight to topple backwards from his knee on to the ground.

Yussef leaned forward as the prince withdrew the rug and Asenath stifled a sob as she saw the hideously contorted features. Yussef held her close for a moment as her shoulders heaved and her tears splashed on to his chest.

'It is over, Princess. It was the only way. His back is broken.'

She struggled to regain mastery of herself and drew away from him, forcing herself to look down at the dead man and then at the set face of his killer. The incident had been so brief and so silent. Hardly a scuffling sound had betrayed their presence. The slave opened the door and hurriedly stepped inside. He took in the situation in a glance.

'The Lord Rehoremheb, is he alive?'

'Yes, lord. He is kept in one of the disused stables.'

'Then we stay only for him. Will you do one more thing for me?'

'Lord.' The man's voice was tense but calm.

'Tell the guard Mardok himself requests the Egyptian's presence here.' He paused and smiled. 'Tell him, Mardok desires that the Egyptian should witness his lady's subjection. That he wishes to see him here, now, in his bed-chamber.'

The man hesitated and the prince said with grim humour, 'Mardok will have no objections.'

The slave cast his former master one glance, then nodded and left the room.

Yussef found himself supporting an almost fainting girl. The horror of Mardok's death had completed Asenath's terror. She could not bear to see the gleam in Mernptah's eyes. Had he enjoyed that? He certainly showed no distaste. He turned back to the business in hand, after giving one dispassionate glance at his betrothed.

'We must be prepared for more action. So far luck or the blessing of the gods, has aided us. Rehoremheb will have an escort. I do not know how many men it will comprise but we must take them by surprise. If one man alerts the household, we are finished.'

Yussef laid the girl back against the velvet cushions. 'I am ready, lord,' he said steadily. 'Can we be sure of the slave?'

'I think so, but we must not take his loyalty for granted. So far he has had little opportunity to betray us, as he has been within distance of my weapon. He will do as I command, I think, I am no light judge of men. He wishes to serve me and his one chance of freedom from this, is with us. Stand on the other side of the door and use your knife fast if you have to.'

The sound of feet coming down the corridor silenced him and he gestured Yussef into position. The door was pushed open and Rehoremheb stumbled into the room. Behind him, the captain of the guard followed leisurely. He was interested to watch this. It was a sport he had not expected to see. The smile hardly had time to die on his lips, as he looked down stupified at the sprawled body of his master. Before he could turn to face the door which clicked to behind him, Mern-ptah had knifed him in the back. He gave a choking gurgle and staggered to his knees. Yussef jerked forward to silence his shout for assistance, but there was no need. The man attempted to talk, reached out a pleading hand, his face both bewildered and childlike, then came a horrible rasping sound, and he was silent.

'Oh may the gods have pity.' Asenath gave a whispered prayer from the bed and Rehoremheb knelt awkwardly to comfort her.

'How many guards outside?' Mern-ptah jerked him to awareness of their peril.

'No one. He brought me alone. He thought Mardok required privacy.' Rehoremheb turned to him with a bitter twist to his lips.

'He did not fear interference.'

The slave had held the door to behind them. He put up one hand now urgently to crave their attention.

'Lords, we must go now at once. The men in the stable will not expect the captain to take long. When he does not return soon with his prisoner, they will come looking.'

'You are right. Nothing now detains us. You are injured, Lord Rehoremheb.' Mern-ptah's eyes flickered to the master builder's right arm which hung awkwardly by his side and which he had not placed round his daughter.

'A sword thrust. It has festered. It pains me but the bleeding has stopped. It does not prevent me walking.'

'The princess . . .' Yussef moved forward, his eyes conveying a warning.

'I must carry her. We will leave by the guest room as we came. There is little use in attempting to hide the bodies; leave them. Check the corridor.'

The slave stepped out and Mern-ptah stooped and lifted Asenath into his arms. It seemed for a moment, that she would resist his effort, then she allowed herself to be held lightly against his shoulder. She could bear no more. She shuddered as she glimpsed one bloodstained hand he had made no effort to cleanse. Even the blessed joy of seeing her father, ill but safe, could not detract from the horror and pain. Her body alternately burned, then seemed icy cold and she felt sick with fear and dread of the man who held her. The slave beckoned them forward and she slipped into blackness as her injured foot jarred against Mern-ptah's thigh.

Mardok's body slave led the way through the darkened guest room, himself checking that the way was clear of servants before beckoning the group on. Mern-ptah strode sure-footed through the room, though he was burdened by Asenath's weight, then they were across the open ground to the shelter of the hedge which separated the house from the tilled fields beyond. Yussef climbed over and took the girl's body from the prince but he insisted on receiving her, once on the other side. Yussef noted with concern that Rehoremheb made no effort to use his right arm in the climb, and he put out a hand to steady him. Rehoremheb disengaged himself afterwards, gently thanking him but saying that he was capable of making the journey without assistance. He looked very pale but Yussef put this down to his concern for Asenath.

The slave led them safely away from the river, waning them of the position of the small irrigation canals into which they might have stumbled in the darkness, unfamiliar as they were, with the terrain.

Mern-ptah had outlined to him his plan to avoid river paths as they would be immediately discovered by their pursuers. The slave knew only the area near to the house, as he had never been allowed freedom to travel, so after the first part of the journey, the prince was forced to rely on his own imperfect remembrance of his journey to Thebes and his knowledge of the plans he had seen in the palace. He judged that the village where he planned to meet Namu and rejoin his ship, was roughly two hours sailing from the house. That meant that it would take the little party until daybreak to reach their destination. To avoid the river and strike inland was simple enough, but the desert was an uncharted waste, where they would lose their way, so it was necessary to keep to the fringe of cultivation, away from the water but sufficiently close to draw conclusions about direction.

No alarm whatever had sounded in the house. As they had passed the garden, he had heard noisy laughter from the stables and outer buildings, where Mardok's foot soldiers were enjoying their off duty hours. It could only be a matter of an hour or less before his death would be discovered. He was sure that the pursuit would be by water and it would take time to fit out a ship. He prayed that time would be long enough for them to get clear. They had of course left tracks, but they would not be easily traced before the morning light.

His eyes had become accustomed to the darkness and he strode on effortlessly, the girl slowing him down not at all. He had wrapped her slightly-clad body in one of the covers, but he was concerned about her condition. Already he could feel the dry burning sensation of her skin through its folds. Once or twice she made little sounds, but she was not coherent. He thanked Ptah, the god of healing, that she was not aware of pain. He forced himself not to think of the consequences of the scorpion sting. He had brought her from the house, somehow he must take her to the palace where Ptah Hoten surely would be able to save her. He felt a strange sense of tightened perception, as though the killings had given him sharpened hearing and sight. He had expected to feel hot anger, but instead steady, cool thought continued and he experienced no panic. He knew this to be the result of training in the battle school. Once danger was over, he would feel the reaction, but for the present, he was concerned only with the leading of the little group to safety. He had no regrets, indeed the swift killing of Mardok had been merely a necessity, not inspired by revenge. Taia's pathetic tale of the massacre at Rehoremheb's house had convinced him of the justice of his action and he knew that by his father's command, when he knew the facts, the remainder of Mardok's officials would receive their deserts.

Rehoremheb stumbled once or twice but pressed resolutely on. The pain in his right arm had worsened but his anxiety was only for the girl in Mern-ptah's arms. Later, when she became delirious and cried out, Yussef begged a halt.

'Lord, we must stay and lay her on the ground. I must look to her condition.'

'To wait now might be suicidal,' the prince raged. 'We must press on.'

'My lord, if you wish to carry a dead princess to Thebes, continue.'

Mern-ptah stopped at once and Yussef drew the fever-wracked girl on to the ground, while the prince supported her head on his knee. He drew his hand away from the dry skin, and tearing off a strip of linen from his robe, moistened it with water from the skin bottle he carried, and wiped her forehead and face and throat. Her eyes were open but unnaturally bright and staring. She breathed in harsh rasping gasps and knew none of them.

'It is as I expected. The fever rages through her body and the events of the night have half crazed her. Lord, I must head for the river. We need more water to bathe her body. Only that way can we hope to reduce this burning fever.'

'To be near the river is to invite capture.'

'It is still dark. If we find a place hidden by the higher papyrus, we might escape detection.'

'Very well I will head for the river. We'll follow the irrigation canal. It seems low in water but it will lead us directly.'

Another hour brought them to an uninhabited stretch of the western bank. There were no houses or huts to be seen but tall papyrus gave the required cover and Yussef made a comfortable bed for her on the crushed rushes and laid her gently down.

'Lord, you must leave the princess with the lord Rehoremheb and I, and go to the village for help. I will do what I can for her. Bring the ship swiftly.'

'But if you are attacked?'

'Lord, we are hidden well and if need arises we will defend ourselves to the end. I am needed here and you only know the position of the boat. You must go. Senta here, Mardok's slave, must accompany you, for if anything happens, one of you must strive to reach the ship.'

Mern-ptah gently laid the girl's head down on the ground and rose. He knew better than to question Yussef's suggestion. He knew she could not survive any further journeying and he was needed to fetch help, yet he was sorely tempted to remain by her side during the critical hours ahead. Yussef and Yussef alone, could aid her now and he did not argue. Rehoremheb was unfit to travel on. Exhaustion showed in his tense face and pale features. Mern-ptah wondered if he had been tortured or kept without food during the days of his captivity.

'I will be back by day-break. The gods grant I come in time.' He touched Asenath's brow with his fingers and was alarmed at its mounting fever. They had no clothes to cover her, or cooling herbs to allay the fever. It was essential that he should convey her to Thebes with all speed, so his mind once made up, he summoned the slave and walked off into the darkness.

Yussef drew water into the skin bottle and stripped the moaning girl. Rehoremheb held her still, while he bathed her body with soaked linen, torn from his robe and administered water when she pleaded huskily for it, through swollen lips. He covered her once more with the silk from Mardok's great bed and sat down to watch and wait.

'The wound on her leg, how did it happen?' Rehoremheb questioned quietly.

'She stood on a scorpion which had entered the bed-chamber while they were preparing her for Mardok's bed. I think she considered it a way out.'

The master builder swallowed and turned away as she tossed and turned under the covers. In her delirium she seemed equally terrified of her abductor and her rescuer, the thought of both seeming to arouse in her horror and dread.

'She does not know what she is saying,' Yussef said stiffly. 'She is shocked by seeing both men killed. When she recovers, she will know of the necessity.'

'*When* she recovers?'

'If the gods will it, otherwise — we must be content.' Yussef's answer was that of the trained healer and Rehoremheb forbore to question further.

'Lord Rehoremheb, your arm. It pains you?' The question was calm but the master builder did not miss the note of concern.

'I think the sword severed a vital muscle or tendon. I am unlikely to use it again,' he said. 'I should not disturb yourself. When I reach Thebes and am confronted by Pharaoh, I am like to lose more than that.'

Yussef drew out his bronze knife from his healer's satchel.

'It will hurt when I cut deep but I can let out the pus and ease the pain,' he said.

Rehoremheb made no fuss while Yussef cleansed the wound and applied a linen bandage on which salve had been spread. 'Could you not take your chance and strike off into the desert, before the prince returns?' he said thoughtfully. 'You can do little here.'

'I cannot leave her.' Rehoremheb's decision was final and Yussef made no effort to dissuade him.

They sat on, their watchful eyes avid for any change in the sick girl's face, and their ears strained for any sound from the river which would indicate the advance of any Hittite soldiers from the house.

16

An hour before the dawn Yussef was conscious of a change in Asenath's condition. Placing a hand on her forehead, he withdrew it wet with sweat.

'The fever is breaking,' he said as Rehoremheb stirred worriedly.

'Will she recover?'

'She has a sound constitution. If her body throws off the poison, she will be well.'

'She is quieter now.'

'For a while she may sleep. In two hours or less it will be light. The ship must arrive by then or I shall fear some accident has happened to the prince.'

'He will return,' Rehoremheb was confident. 'He is the son of his father.'

'My lord, will you not reconsider your decision of last night? Now may be your only hope. She will be safe with me.'

A brief smile touched the master builder's lips. 'I shall not leave her again until,' he hesitated, 'until I am forced to. Even now she may need me.'

'So be it, lord.' Yussef broke off, as his ears had caught a sound from the river.

Rehoremheb jumped up. In the distance they could hear a splashing of water and voices calling. Mindful of the danger, Rehoremheb gestured to Yussef to remain where he was and indicated a place further along the bank where he would be able to view the expanse of water, which stretched behind them to the house they had left. Yussef and the princess were obscured by the reeds. From the bank they would not be discernible.

It seemed an age while the noise of men's voices drew nearer. He was relieved to discover a largish pleasure boat. The nobles, who sat beneath its awning, had obviously been guests at a party. They were still merry from the feasting, and were doubtless returning to their own homes. As if awakened by the noise their voices made, Asenath opened her eyes and then roused herself and gazed searchingly round.

'He is safe, Princess. He has gone to find the ship. Rehoremheb is down at the river to investigate the source of the noise. It is only some tipsy revellers. There is nothing to fear.'

The concern faded from her eyes and she reached out for Yussef's hand. He was pleased to note that the clamminess and burning had gone. Her voice was a little husky, though loud enough to carry.

'He will return soon?'

'I expect him in an hour or at the most two. Are you in pain, Princess? How is the wound?'

She moved experimentally then flushed as she found herself naked beneath the covers.

'It is sore but better.'

Yussef was gravely courteous. 'You were fevered, lady. It was necessary that I should bathe you. It was a healer's privilege. It meant nothing.'

She turned away and he saw a glimmer of tears in her eyes but she put up a bared arm to dash them away. 'It is nothing, Yussef. It is weakness nothing else. Dear Yussef, you have always been so good to me. Why did you risk yourself?'

'Do you need to ask?'

She turned a troubled gaze to his serious face.

'He knows?'

'I think he does.'

'Oh Yussef what will he do to me? I am so afraid of him.'

'Yet your first thought was for his safety.' The healer's voice was somewhat bitter and she touched his hand again fleetingly.

'Yussef, part of my heart will always be yours. You must believe me. I did not wilfully play with you that day — or if I did, it was not so later, truly. All my concern was for you. I cannot help that I . . .' Tears threatened to choke her again and he comforted her with the pressure of his fingers on her small hand.

'Lady, I will worship you always. There is no cause for you to feel ashamed. I know you love him. If I doubted it, those doubts were dispelled when we entered Mardok's bed-chamber. You loved him then and you will always do so. You ached for him, longed for him to come, yet your first words commanded him to leave you.'

'Yet I fear him.'

'Lady, you must realize the necessity which prompted him to destroy those men. Had he given them time to defend themselves, the alarm would have been given. It was his prompt actions which have saved us all. Would you have had the master builder dead or in a foreign slave market because Mern-ptah had pity or stopped to consider what was honourable conduct?'

She swallowed convulsively. 'You chide me with good reason, friend, but you misunderstand. *I* am the guilty one. None of us would have been in peril, but for my foolish conduct. Do you think he will forgive that?'

'You will have to endure punishment, lady. You will not be alone.'

Her gaze followed his to the river bank where Rehoremheb could be heard splashing in the water, cleansing his body of the odour of dirt and sweat which had sickened his fastidious person, during the days of captivity.

'My father, he will punish him.' Until now the full horror of his danger had not dawned on her.

'The gods have already done so. It is likely he will lose his right arm.'

'Oh no, Yussef, you cannot mean that. He is an architect, a designer, he needs to draw his plans. The gods wreak punishment on me who has brought about this.'

'Lady, have courage. We will win through. You must find the right words to speak to your brother. He only, will know how to plead for the master builder. In the night he could have fled, but he would not leave you.'

Rehoremheb looked worriedly at the others, when some time later, they heard the splash of oars and knew a ship was approaching. He stood up and moved closer to the bank.

'Is it the prince?' Yussef spoke softly, while he placed one comforting hand on the princess's arm.

'I think it is, they are pulling in. Yes I'm sure of it. He has sprung ashore. He's coming.'

Anxiety had sharpened Mern-ptah's features, when he pushed back the reeds and looked down at them. His relief was apparent when he saw Asenath's troubled eyes look up at him.

'So you are better. It is well, for I want us embarked without loss of time. Have you had trouble?' His question was directed at Yussef, who shook his head.

'No sign of pursuit. Either they went downstream or made no attempt at all to follow.'

'With Mardok dead, they lost heart I imagine.' Mern-ptah stooped and lifted the sick girl. 'Come, Namu waits and I wish to be in Thebes before river traffic builds up.'

Asenath felt the strong beat of his heart against her own breast. He had made little effort to talk to her and she was thankful to escape censure for the time being, though knew a reckoning would be demanded later. He strode easily forward and set her down on the deck, while he clambered aboard. She waved away Yussef, who sprang on board quickly, anxious to come to her assistance, and stood up. She felt faint at first but already normal colour was flooding her cheeks and she knew she would quickly recover. That the master builder was in great pain was becoming increasingly obvious to them all. Their new slave sat with Reuben in the prow and Yussef moved quietly to join them.

Asenath sat silently on deck, leaning against Rehoremheb's shoulder. He stroked her bright hair with his uninjured hand and she tried to check the tears which splashed on to her knee as she stared at Mern-ptah's back, turned unresponsively from her. She could not bear to talk to Rehoremheb or offer him encouragement. She was sure of nothing and now in the early cold chill of the dawn, the full horror of guilt burst upon her. She had shamed the family honour, risked the lives of those who loved her, and brought her own father close to destruction. She could find no excuse for her conduct, and the folly of her escape from the Great House could not be explained. She had behaved like a spoilt, stupid child. If only she could have been punished like a child, without the dire consequences she feared.

All too soon, Thebes came into sight and already river traffic was getting thicker. Workmen were crossing on the ferry to begin the day's labour, and respectful salutes were offered to the royal prince, who stood unsmiling on deck. He instructed Namu to tie up at the royal landing stage and stepped forward to assist him in the manœuvre.

Asenath forced herself to be calm as the ship stood at rest and he turned back to her.

'Can you walk? It will excite less comment if you can do so.'

'Yes,' her voice was husky but calm, 'yes, I can do so.'

He held out his hand and she timidly placed her own within it, as he drew her lightly ashore. She drew the silken cover round her scantily-clad form and hurried with him through the garden. They both halted abruptly as Pharaoh stepped from his private apartment to confront them. His eyes were as tortured as Mern-ptah's had been, as he looked from his son to his adopted daughter. She looked at him pleadingly, her lovely eyes brimming with tears, and silently he opened his arms to her. She threw herself forward and sobbed brokenly against his bared chest. Over her bowed head, Pharaoh smiled and nodded to his son. Mern-ptah bowed and left them.

Gently Pharaoh drew her away from him and tilted up her chin. 'So the runaway has returned.'

'Oh my father — oh . . .'

'Do not talk. Now is not the time. Go to Serana. Her heart is torn with worry. I will hear your story later.'

She sought to detain him but he impelled her commandingly towards the palace and she could do nothing but obey.

At the landing stage Pharaoh's gaze swept the ship. Namu at once stopped his work of taking in sail but he waved him to continue. Reuben touched the Hittite slave's elbow and bowing low, lead the way through the gardens to the slave quarters. Yussef's troubled gaze passed from the great ruler himself to his master builder. He started, as he saw the fierce black eyes fixed on him and hurried to prostrate himself.

'Await me in my private apartment. I think you know the way.' Yussef rose and gave one last look at the injured man, then slowly moved away.

Rehoremheb did not take his gaze from Pharaoh. He clumsily made to fall to the ground but the familiar harsh voice arrested him.

'Captain, convey the lord Rehoremheb to the Temple of Ptah. He needs attention.'

'I think it is hardly worth the High Priest's trouble,' Rehoremheb said, his mouth twisting wryly, 'but I thank you.'

'Why?' The question was thrown at him and he shrugged in answer.

'I had no choice. I do not offer that as an excuse. You know her. You knew her mother. She would have gone alone, and I could not let her do that.'

Pharaoh's grim expression relaxed. A slight smile hovered about his lips. He nodded. 'So, it is as you say. Go now and have your hurts attended to.'

'You swear she will be safe?'

'Can you doubt it?'

'She is afraid of him.'

'She has good cause, but he loves her well. Neither of us can interfere now. Asenath is his problem, and I think he has begun well.'

Rehoremheb bowed his head and giving the royal salute, turned away.

Yussef stood in Pharaoh's apartment, staring unseeingly across the garden. His mouth was a little dry. His last interview with the lord of The Two Lands had not been a pleasant one. He turned anxiously as Pharaoh entered alone and closed the door. He stood for a moment, a frown creasing his brow while he gazed long at the young healer.

'What will you do?' he said at last.

'Lord?' The word was a question.

'It is clear that you love her. What will you do?'

Dull colour suffused Yussef's cheeks. 'I do not know, but I will endure. She is safe, that is all that matters.'

Again Pharaoh was silent. He seated himself and indicated a stool for the former slave.

'I would wish to do something for you. You have your freedom. You will need money. I understand you wish to be a physician. I could arrange an apprenticeship with one of the most celebrated physicians in Thebes. This would please you?'

'Lord, I thank you with a full heart . . .

but, but I think it will be better if soon I leave Thebes. I have long considered the possibility of entering Temple service permanently. The Temple of Ptah in Memphis would take me as an acolyte. When I am sure and they are willing to accept me, I could aspire to enter the priesthood here.'

'You are wise I think. Yussef, do not seek the service of the god as an escape from your suffering. I am an initiate priest. I know what I say.'

'I understand, lord.'

'My son will miss you. I think he loves you well.'

'He will know the need for my decision.'

Pharaoh smiled and rose. 'I wish I could offer you comfort.'

'Lord you can do so if you assure me that the princess will not be punished.'

The smile deepened round Pharaoh's mobile mouth. 'That I cannot do. The matter is out of my hands. Mern-ptah will be her husband. He will know how to discipline his wife. I know my son. I do not think she will behave so again. Return to Ptah Hoten. He may need you at the Temple. I think it may prove necessary to operate on Lord Rehoremheb. I have deep affection for the man. I would know that he has the very best attention in Thebes.'

Yussef's face was suddenly illumined. He stooped to kiss Pharaoh's sandal thong and turned to leave.

'I hope that one day, when Mern-ptah wears the double crown, he will have a healer he can trust, as truly as I trust mine.'

'It shall be so, lord. I swear it. Nothing will ever come between my love for him — nothing.' The frown had left Pharaoh's face when he went, but he sat on thoughtful, tapping one hand against his knee, then he sighed and went in search of his wife.

Serana came to him and he took her hands and squeezed them hard.

'Well?'

'She is not touched.'

'You are sure? Mern-ptah says he did not question her.'

'I have done so. All is well.'

He expelled a sigh of relief. 'I confess I was disturbed. He is determined to marry her — but had she become pregnant . . .'

Serana turned away her head. Only too well she had known the horror and terror which followed a discovery such as he feared. The knowledge she was to bear Pharaoh a child, had not brought her pleasure. Only later, had she discovered supreme happiness in his arms. She had dreaded to question her stepdaughter, but had known the necessity.

'I must speak with her,' he said quietly.

She nodded. 'Be gentle with her, lord. She has suffered enough for the present.'

Asenath was resting on her stepmother's bed. Her mother's ladies had bathed her and clothed her in a simple linen dress. Serana herself had comforted and fed her, gently insisting when Asenath had begged her to send away the food. She stood up at once at Pharaoh's entrance.

'Be seated, child. You are better?'

She nodded, flushing at the grave but solicitious tone of his voice.

'Mern-ptah tells me you suffered a scorpion sting. You are fortunate to be recovered.'

'My father I know that but for the courage of others I would not be here now. I am ashamed that I caused so much trouble.'

'I am glad you are aware of the seriousness of your conduct. However, that is in the past. We must talk now of the future. Your mother tells me that you are still a virgin.'

Asenath lowered her head. Her father had never before spoken to her of intimate matters. He continued. 'It relieves my mind, however your behaviour might still cause comment if it were commonly known. I will ask you one question and one only. Are you prepared to marry Mern-ptah?'

As she made to answer, he checked her by raising his hand. 'Let me finish. If you choose not to do so, you must understand that you cannot continue to live here at court. I will send you away with attendants where you may live quietly until we can find a husband for you, more to your liking. Having considered the matter, I feel that undue pressure from me forced you to behave as you did. When I was young, princes and princesses did not seek to please themselves in such matters.'

Asenath did not dare look at him. She was very close to tears. 'It is for Mern-ptah now to say if he will take me as his bride. If he will overlook this incident, I am ready to do whatever you wish, my father.'

Pharaoh leaned forward and took her cold hands.

'Mern-ptah is anxious that the ceremony shall take place without delay. I may arrange it for the day after tomorrow then? There will be no more scenes? Once you are his wife, it will be for him to see that you obey.'

'I swear to you, my father, that I will make every effort to do what he requires of me.'

'H'm.' He stood up smiling a little. 'I imagine he will be most pleased when you provide him with an heir as soon as possible.'

'Rehoremheb?' Her voice was pleading, very low.

'I shall not punish him. I am concerned about his wound. I wait to hear from the Temple if he is to lose the arm. When I hear news, I will send and inform you. Now, you must rest and allow your ladies to do their best to restore your beauty. Mern-ptah will wish to see you completely restored in health and beauty, when he makes you his bride.'

17

Yussef was busy in the store-room of the Temple when Ptah Hoten's form blotted out the light from the doorway, and he turned at once, anxious to obey the High Priest in whatever he commanded.

'Go to my own apartment, Yussef, there is one who wishes to see you.'

Yussef was puzzled. Visitors were rare and he doubted if Mern-ptah would come today to see him. By noon he would be publicly united to Asenath and he would be busy, preparing himself. They had said their farewells the day before. Soon he would leave for Memphis to undergo a period of training before it was decided whether he was suitable to enter the priesthood. They had said little to each other. Each knew the other's mind and respected his reasons. Later, when Yussef's wound was less raw, they would meet again. Perhaps Reuben had been spared for a while, yet even he would be busily engaged on this day.

He stopped still in the doorway as he saw her. Even her straight proud little back was dear to his eyes. She had not heard the soft patter of his reed sandals, but at last she turned and regarded him intently.

'I could not let you go, without bidding you goodbye. I knew you would not come to me.'

He moved forward, quiet for a moment, because there was little to say.

'I thank the gods that I have this moment to wish you happiness, Princess,' he said at last. The formality of the words could not hide their true sincerity and she leaned forward and took his hand.

'You know that I love him — I want so much to know that all will be well with you, Yussef.'

'All will be well, lady. They have told you I intend to enter the priesthood?'

'Yes. You are a true healer, Yussef. In this service you will find happiness.'

'As you will, lady. When you sit beside him on the throne, I shall know that his wisest decrees will be drawn up, with your help.'

She shook her head, a faint smile touching her lips. 'Mern-ptah will make his own decisions. It will be for me to obey. My part will be to provide him with an heir and to be patient when he seeks distraction from his other women. I think, Yussef, I would have had a greater chance of happiness had I been your wife. Like all of us, I must settle for what happiness the gods choose to grant me. He is all my joy.'

'Princess I shall never forget what you have just said. I am honoured and proud that I have served you.'

'May your god grant you the love you deserve,' she said softly. 'I will think of you often and I pray we shall meet again, when the time is ripe.'

He crossed to the window and stood staring out over the courtyard. She had gone and for a while he could not force himself to meet the serene gaze of his priestly masters. The sun was not yet high but already he knew the poor would be entering at the pylon; the lame, those whose eyes were sore with the common affliction of the peasants, those whose patient expressions spoke of suffering long and courageously endured. He would be needed in the healing ward, for already he had learned much and the healers had need of his services. In hard work he could forget the agony of his love for her who was out of his reach. He prayed that the Royal Heir would give her the happiness she craved.

After her ladies had left her, Asenath stood by the open doorway to the apartment to breathe in the night air. It had been a glittering ceremony which had made her Great Wife of the Royal Heir, Daughter of Isis indeed.

Rehoremheb had smiled encouragingly at her during the feast which followed. Ptah Hoten had pronounced that Yussef's prompt action with the knife, had saved the master builder's arm, but it would always hang limp by his side. A tendon had been cut and it was doubtful if he would ever again with it aim a throwing stick at the water fowl on the Nile, or draw a plan for a new temple.

Now she awaited Mern-ptah's summons. From the doorway, she could see the gay pennants of the Temple of Ptah fluttering over the tops of the trees in the garden. Tonight Thebes was aglow with torches and lighted brands. The townsfolk were celebrating her marriage. She could hear them laughing and singing in the streets. Yussef would not be of their number. Soon it would be the hour for evening celebrations. He was not yet a priest but at the sound of the priestesses' systra, and chanting, he would pause in his work of healing in silent contemplation of the God who gave all life and form. She knew he would put her out of his heart. It was necessary. Her affection for him was a pure warm glow, in contrast to the strange longing yet fear of her husband which sent her heart pounding and turned her limbs to water at his approach.

She had seen little of him since his rescue of her. Preparations for the marriage had taken up all of their time. He had been courteous, solicitous of her well-being, but they had not been alone together once. She dreaded the moment when it would be so. Now she was his wife, his property and he could do with her as he chose.

She turned at once when the inner door was softly opened, expecting to see Memnet, who would tell her of the expected summons. He stood there, his back to the closed door. He caught his breath at her unadorned loveliness. Clad in the finest of mist-linen she looked hardly real, as the oil lamp glimmered on the bronze of her hair, free now from its ceremonial wig and golden headdress. Her sandals were studded with gold and she wore only a golden snake bracelet round her right arm.

He came quietly to her side and put his arm possessively round her waist, while he looked past her into the garden.

'He has chosen his part, my wife,' he said gently, 'as we must play ours.'

She nodded and turned to look full at him. His fierce face was unusually softened, and she found herself staring at the scar which still stood out starkly on his smooth tanned cheek. She averted her eyes abruptly. 'You are unattended?' she questioned him.

'Of course.' His answer was half amused.

'I . . . I . . . thought you would send for me.'

'I thought you would prefer that I came.'

'Yes . . . I do.' Again he found it difficult to catch her answer.

He held her at arms length for a moment. 'Are you afraid?'

She smiled. 'A little.'

'It is how it should be, but you need not be.'

She lifted one hand and ran her finger lightly down the scar. 'But when do I pay for this?'

He smiled crookedly. 'Some debts wait long to be collected, my wife. Some are even forgiven and never collected at all. Perhaps it will be so with you.' Then he lifted her up into his arms and she gave a little sigh of content. The night was young and the revellers would roister for hours yet, in the streets. It would be aeons of time before the Royal Heir and his bride would have to face attendants. Suddenly the court seemed very far away, and all Egypt cut off from the heaven of her small room.

We hope you have enjoyed this Large Print book. Other G.K. Hall or Chivers Press Large Print books are available at your library or directly from the publishers.

For more information about current and upcoming titles, please call or write, without obligation, to:

G.K. Hall
P.O. Box 159
Thorndike, Maine 04986
USA
Tel. (800) 223-2336

OR

Chivers Press Limited
Windsor Bridge Road
Bath BA2 3AX
England
Tel. (0225) 335336

All our Large Print titles are designed for easy reading, and all our books are made to last.